Praise for
Kat

"Funny, sharp as hell."

— Adam McKay, director of *Don't Look Up* and *The Big Short*

"*Kill the Rich* is like a portrayal of what remains after the third horse of the apocalypse gets lost during a coke binge while documenting its journey through the desert wilderness for its Insta feed. The novel rides easily between farce and satire by savaging the absurdities of our moment, both culturally and politically, and takes us on a ride through the nightmare landscape we worry lurks around the corner. Only writers with comic vision and guts like Allison and Shapiro could get us to the end of this tale."

— Joe Milan Jr., author of *The All-American*

"*Kill the Rich* is a hilarious hell ride through what feels like an increasingly possible future. Kate and Jack portray a world steeped in biting absurdism— one which can easily be recognized as an outgrowth of present day reality."

— Mira Gonzalez, author of *I Will Never Be Beautiful Enough to Make Us Beautiful Together*

"Crafting great dystopian fiction is a task that seems nearly impossible in our dystopian, fake-seeming world, but Allison and Shapiro have managed to do just that. Gripping, hilarious, and brimming with humanity. The fact that it all feels so authentic, plausible, and downright subtle is the book's most unsettling victory."

— JASON WOLINER, DIRECTOR OF *BORAT SUBSEQUENT MOVIEFILM* AND *PAUL T. GOLDMAN*

Kill The Rich

Jack Allison

Kate Shapiro

CLASH

Cover by Joel Amat Güell

Troy, NY

CLASH Books

clashbooks.com

To the 1%, may you live long and healthy lives

The Free America Act

Sponsor: Rep. Mariana Ortiz (APP-FL)

Committees: Financial Services; Energy and Commerce; Judiciary; Rules; Budget; Oversight and Government Reform; Ways and Means

The Free America Act authorizes the Department of Justice to set criminal penalties up to and including capital punishment for individuals whose companies engage in (1) money laundering (2) anti-competitive actions (3) Wall Street speculation (4) environmental code violations (5) corporate espionage and (6) fraud.

One

"The Age of Disorder is likely upon us. In the years ahead, simply extrapolating past trends could be the biggest mistake you make."
—Jim Reid, Deutsche Bank

June 18, 2038 | Washington, D.C.

Jay Betteta felt good. A blonde lobbyist twink lay in the bed with his vape still halfway in his mouth. D.C. was sometimes magical in that it was not Arlington Texas—Jay's hometown where the typical Grindr gay was a pudgy, pale torso of a man you later found out was a pastor who said the N-word when he came. People here may be bad on the inside, but at least they looked good on the outside.

His phone buzzed.

CNNBC Alert: House fails to end Federal death penalty to stay Kardashian execution.

Jay whistled and slipped his phone into his messenger bag. He pulled tight a Full-Windsor knot. Usually, he made do with a

Half, but today he wanted to look his best. The blonde woke up and mumbled, asking if Jay wanted to get brunch.

"Out," Jay told him. Today was a big day.

Today they were going to kill Kim Kardashian.

A well-dressed man transported a powder from a plastic baggie into capsules on the 57 bus. A woman wore a t-shirt emblazoned with Pablo's iconic "Kill the Rich" campaign logo in sepia serif font against maroon, certainly on her way to the event on the National Mall—Jay's idea—where artists, activists, and musicians would hold a day-long block party to benefit the victims of Kim Kardashian.

His phone rang, and he swiped to answer.

"Are you screening my calls?" demanded Lupe from the other end. He could hear the hum of the West Wing in the background around her. Cell phones, typing, frenzied conversations. "I'm the Chief of Staff of the fucking White House, Jay. You don't screen my calls."

"I'm sorry, Lupe," he said, "I was walking to the bus stop and must have missed the call."

"Why can't you just get a Pegasus like the rest of us? It's a *security concern*," she grumbled, referring to the Loots self-driving car contract for White House members to get to work without interacting with the unwashed masses.

He started to explain, once again, why he didn't trust the electric car meme guy Willem Loots's self-driving cars with nearly 3,000 reported pedestrian accidents, but he long ago discovered Lupe Fox had selective hearing. Especially when it came to wealthy people with government contracts.

As a young man in the 2020s, Jay thought Rep. Lupe Fox's TikTok Senate explainers were going to change the world. He felt a parasocial kinship with her, as a homeless orphan living out of his car. Her journey from a waitress at the Spaghetti Warehouse to Congress to the Senate gave him *hope*, a rare commodity in the twenty-first century. When he joined Pablo's campaign, he found that most of that persona he admired so much was written by a consulting firm and that she had only worked as a waitress for a month during a summer break from Brown. She endorsed Pablo when it was clear he was going to win and joined his campaign, promising him she'd be a bridge to Congress, an insider on *his* side. The jury was out on that one, Jay thought.

In the background, he heard Pablo say: is he at home? Tell him to grab me a breakfast sandwich from the cart. Lupe dutifully relayed the message. "POTUS wants a breakfast sandwich."

"Hot sauce?" Jay asked.

Extra, Pablo added as the bus pulled up. Lupe was about to ask for another confirmation when Jay apologized and hung up. Lupe needed triplicate confirmation for everything. The power dynamics of D.C. often cast a dissociative pall over Jay. Was he doing something wrong? Was she trying to tell him something in the repeating of a breakfast order?

Someone pulled the cord and as the bus pulled to a stop outside the White House, a woman in an ill-fitting Ann Taylor suit, zipper just barely fitting over her middle-aged paunch, stepped in his way.

The woman roared his name and shoved a glossy photograph into his hand. Jay squinted at a photograph of Kim Kardashian's children, teenagers and young adults now, all on the red carpet together in exorbitantly expensive outfits for their television show, *Kim's Brood*. Even her children were products.

"Look at them. You're making them orphans," she said, though their fathers were all alive and well. She sprayed something into his face and mouth, stinging his eyes. At first, he thought it was pepper spray, and then when the pain didn't come but instead, the smell of lilacs and polyester thongs, he thought: Kim Kardashian body mist.

"Smell her. Remember her," she said, then let him pass.

"Don't mind her," the girl in the Kill The Rich t-shirt said. "You're a hero," she said, patting his arm. He smiled at her.

Off the bus, he wiped the perfume from his face and watched his attacker join a modest group of pro-Kim protesters gathering near the Washington Monument, the perennially under-construction penis in the sky.

A small but loud group of women decried the attack on Kim as an attack on women, saying that plenty of *men* destroyed the environment without being executed (even though just last year, they had executed the last remaining beyond-geriatric Koch brother, it just got low ratings), and that Kim's treatment was sexist and inhumane. It was amazing, Jay thought, how people gathered together to support people they had never met, people who actively *hated* them, and just let the people in their own life burn.

He knew this firsthand. His own mother had burned on account of a rich person, his father, who left them with nothing to start a new white family and pharma start-up in Phoenix's burgeoning tech alley. His mother never truly recovered from that. More to the point, she never recovered from the cancer that Jay's father refused to contribute money to treat.

On the sidewalk, so close to the White House as to be brazen, there was a long line of homeless people waiting at a table with signage that read "FREE BUS TO LOOTS TOWN." More hopeless people, lining up for the chance to burn on account of another rich person.

Jay shook it off. He looked at the picture of Kim's family. In Jay's experience, being an orphan was preferable to a world full of people like Kim Kardashian and his father. He balled it up, threw it into a trash can, and walked towards the White House.

"These Beltway fuckers want a world that doesn't exist anymore," President Pablo Lopez said, pacing the perimeter of the Oval. He picked up a small statue of a horse and examined it. "What even is this? Why is the Oval Office filled with all this dumb knick-knack tchotchke shit? I'm the leader of the free world, why does my office feel like a fucking Bennigan's?" He firmly pressed the strange small horse back onto its obscene ivory pedestal.

"You know why it doesn't exist? Because they killed it! I didn't kill it. I'm trying to fucking save it! But these people, these fucking people, they go on TV and call me difficult. All smiles to my face and then these Democratic-Republican *fucks* go on CNNBC and call me Stalin! It's disgusting. They say they love the American people and then pass bills to put them in fucking bankruptcy. I just can't. Where the fuck is Jay?"

"Right here," Jay responded, standing near the door at Lupe's side. He'd managed a stealthy entrance a moment earlier while Pablo was in the kind of ranting fugue state he went into when he was under extreme pressure. The Nixon tapes seemed a lot less unhinged when you worked in the actual Oval Office.

"You're in charge of messaging. What are you saying to counter the story that I'm a mother-killer?" he said. The Koch brother was one thing—he was old and had a Wikipedia with a "Controversy" section that was like an endless scroll. Kim was a household name that people grew up with. People had Kim Kardashian shampoo in their shower. Jay explained that they had explainer videos going out on their socials from the real people who had been disfigured, destroyed, and poisoned by Kim's greed. The Secretary of the Interior was doing a roadshow.

"You really shouldn't turn on cable news, today of all days," Jay soothed. He eyed Lupe, who held up her pug to her phone, snapping photos for Bring Your Dog to Work Day.

"You're right. Fucking *nerves*. Where's my breakfast sandwich?" Pablo asked, turning his full magnetic force in Jay's direction. There was nothing in the President's features that suggested he was attractive. In fact, he would probably be ugly if he were anyone but Pablo Lopez. He was sturdy but slightly overweight, with the beginnings of a middle-age gut. His hair was wild and unkempt, which forced him to constantly sweep it away from his eyes (Magnus Ferrell had made a meal of that tic on Saturday Night Live). He was starting to gray around the temples and in flecks in his full mustache. His eyes were small and dark, and too far apart, and his lips were too small. But somehow, when it all fit together, it worked for him. There was something about this asymmetrical former roofer that reminded

Americans of themselves, but slightly hotter, which is really what Americans loved more than anything.

Jay handed the sandwich over. Pablo unwrapped it, took a bite, then sniffed at it.

"A Kim psycho sprayed body mist on me,"

"We don't use the word psycho," Lupe said, putting the dog down.

"A Kim *supporter* sprayed body mist on me," Jay corrected. Pablo laughed, shrugged, and took a bite of the sandwich.

An assistant knocked and poked her head in the door. "Sir, they're on line one," she said.

"Transfer it to Jay," Pablo said, mouth full of egg. He turned to Jay with a puppy-dog look in his eyes.

"No. Come on," Jay said.

"Sorry, buddy. This is senior advisor shit. You can do this." He clapped Jay on the back.

Jay paced the Rose Garden, cell phone to his ear as he waited for Senate Majority Leader Jacky Cohn to join on the other end. D.C. people had the annoying habit of putting you on hold even when *they* were the one who placed the call.

"I've got Majority Leader Cohn," the Adderalled-out voice of the Senate intern on the other end said.

"Put her through."

Jay could hear the heavy breath of the octogenarian Senator on the other end before she finally spoke. "Ch-avier," she always spoke his name with a hard CH. "We need the President to stay the execution."

"We can't do that, Senator Cohn. Kardashian lost her appeal. Take it up with the courts."

Cohn sighed; Jay recoiled at the shuddering hiss on the line. "People are scared, Javier. This is—"

He finished the Democratic-Republican rallying cry in unison with her: "...not who we are."

"This is serious, Jay. You should hear the calls my office is getting. No one wants to return to the horrifying days of the Second Civil War."

Jay couldn't help but roll his eyes. The so-called "Second Civil War" was such a joke. A bunch of LARPers in rascal scooters wandering around State Capitols. Sure, they'd been able to get some compelling television out of it—CNNBC embeds with helmets breathlessly reporting like it was Baghdad while fart machines went off in the background, Anderson Cooper crying on air about "Another day that will live in infamy." In reality, less than 20 people died in the sequel to the Civil War drummed up by cable news. Most of them were excitement-induced heart attacks. It wasn't a real Civil War; it was New Journalism from deep cable channels desperate for one last gasp of ratings and relevancy. The only concrete thing it did was unite the legacy Democratic and Republican parties into a single entity of "conventional wisdom" and "sensible politics"—the Democratic-Republicans (it didn't hurt that the name called to mind a memorable moment from the classic play *Hamilton*)—in opposition to the new parties: the progressive American People's Party and the hard-right conspiracy-obsessed Patriotic Party.

"Despite what your rich donors are tying up your phones with," Jay responded, "this is far from dividing us into another fake Civil War." He couldn't help but get a jab in. "This thing polls above fifty. *Nothing* polls above fifty these days. Besides, why do you need us? I thought you guys were going to stay the execution up on the Hill." Jay grinned. "It seems like you didn't have the votes."

Cohn clicked her tongue. The American People's Party used the floor time to tout the anti-monopoly measures in the Free America Act and the Patriotic Party used it to wonder if the President was even executing the *real* Kim Kardashian.

"So, I'm sorry, what are we even talking about then? You don't have the votes, we're moving forward with the execution. Why are we still on the phone?"

"*Because*, Javier, you don't know how this will poll five months from now in the midterms. There are vulnerable members in your caucus and now your opponents can show a brutal ISIS-K style execution in their campaign ads."

A threat, Jay thought. "The execution is happening. That's a non-starter. But is there anything else I can help you out with?"

Jay could hear a smile crawl across her face over the phone line. Everything up until now had been foreplay for this moment: "I have a very talented great-nephew," Cohn continued. "I think he'd make a great addition to the State Department."

Jay closed his eyes, hating this town. But it was all worth it to pull off the day's festivities with Cohn's tacit approval. "Deal."

"Let's go over the speech," Jay said, handing Lupe and Pablo printouts as the motorcade raced through Metro D.C. "I feel like we really need to nail the why of what we're doing here before you're on camera."

Pablo sighed. He hated rehearsing. "'My parents, like so many before them, came to this country for the opportunity to build a life for themselves and their children. Their small electronics repair shop was never going to be listed on the NYSE, but it was the backbone of Main Street in Arlington, Texas," Pablo stopped. "Fucking Main Street on Arlington, Texas is a water park and four pro sports stadiums, really?"

"It's a performance, Pablo, be your relatable self," Lupe said.

Pablo grumbled then continued: "However, my parents and so many others were irrevocably damaged by the unbridled greed of major corporations that sought to destroy competition no matter how small," Pablo said. This Jay knew to be true. Pablo's father's small grocery was bankrupted by a 24-hour Walmart undercutting his prices. Pablo's family had to close the business and get jobs in ridesharing to put food on the table. A table Jay often sat at.

"Now, my political rivals and the corporate media mouthpieces on CNNBC and Fox News will try to paint this as an assault on successful people, but they know, we know, that Kim

Kardashian is not an innocent woman," he read. Jay was convinced that the thing that won Pablo the Presidency (with only a third of the vote in a crowded election, but still) was the way he spoke. He illustrated his points with animated hand gestures. He seemed like your best friend. Your cool uncle. Someone who you could—really, actually—*have a beer with.* Not like the Ivy League clones they'd said that about before who'd wince at the first sip and count every carb.

"'She would've gotten away with all of it if it weren't for one brave whistleblower. We all owe a great debt of gratitude to Ms. Kardashian's former personal assistant," Pablo said, then paused. "Do we remember her name?" he asked.

Lupe scrolled through her iPad then said: "Sasha Ivanov."

"Is she going to be there?"

"She's bad on TV," Lupe said. "Almost fucked up the entire case on the stand. I can show it to you on YouTube if you want." She started to pull up the video on her tablet, but Pablo shook his head. He raced through the rest of the speech and then sat, eyes still closed, considering the words.

"Good. It's good. I think it's good," he said finally. Lupe nodded along. "But let's cut the part about directing the DOJ to go aggressive on the Free America Act. I don't want to get called a flip-flopper if we don't do another one of these."

"Good call," Lupe said. Her office had developed an exhaustive report on how Kim Kardashian's execution was enough for the midterms. Sure, it polled well but how much death was too much death? Pablo was more and more often deferring to her and her pollsters and social listeners on policy even though, in Jay's opinion, high-paid "pollsters and social listeners" who lived on Twitter were what forced the country towards public executions on C-SPAN in the first place.

Jay opened a presentation he had saved on his tablet. "On that subject," he said, sidling up next to Pablo. "I've been wanting to talk to you about Willem Loots. Did you know this motherfucker has got people working his land, unpaid, like he's some kind of feudal lord?"

"Jay, with all due respect," interrupted Lupe, "can we get

through with today before we move on to your next target? A climate warrior at that."

"Lupe, with all due respect," Jay retorted, handing Pablo the tablet. "Have you seen this tweet?"

***@WillemLoots**: I challenge President Lopez to single combat for the life of Kim Kardashian. If this is a guillotine world, I propose guillotine rules.*

The motherfucker challenged the President to a fucking fist fight. The President *had* to respond to an overt threat of harm to his person.

"The guy is a fucking edgelord, always has been," Lupe said. "It's harmless."

"I'm with Lupe," Pablo said. "I don't have the bandwidth for this right now." Pablo caught the quick flash of hurt across Jay's face and added, "Let's see how today goes, and then we'll talk about this. I promise."

They sat in silence for the remainder of the ride as Pablo went through the speech again making small tweaks.

When you travel with the President, you always end up in some kind of embarrassing little parade. A gaggle of reporters and photographers followed closely behind the two of them, asking questions and snapping pictures.

The procession came to an end as they reached their destination. A barred door buzzed and then slid aside, and Pablo stepped into the holding area. Before him, behind another set of bars, sat reality show star, entrepreneur, and mass man-slaughterer Kim Kardashian.

Jay noted that it seemed she had aged decades overnight. The 57-year-old media mogul who had managed to look 25 her entire life now looked *old*. She'd gained weight from the prison food. Without access to Botox, her face sagged. She had bags under her eyes. Her face was expressionless. Her implants looked strange in the orange jumpsuit, mutated and hard. She sat, lumpy, with a bag of McDonald's breakfast at her side, presumably her final meal request. She looked different, almost like a normal person.

But she wasn't. Jay knew that. She stood for everything that held Americans back for thirty years. Tax loopholes. Environmental disasters. Monopolies. Crushing dissenters. She was a part of the reason "Kill the Rich" became a rallying cry in the first place. A symbol graffitied on buildings and flown on flags.

Pablo stood as the photographers snapped photos and the journalists scribbled down notes, regarding Kardashian silently with a rehearsed expression that Lupe said should read "compassionate but determined." One of the few things that Lupe and Jay agreed on was the necessity of such a big performance—the President couldn't appear bloodthirsty.

Pablo closed his eyes and made a small sign of the cross on his chest and then wordlessly left the room. The crowd of aides and press followed, and Jay stayed behind in their wake. He found himself alone with the woman he had worked so hard to put to death.

"Can I help you?" she said, unwrapping her McGriddle.

"My name is Javier Betteta. I work with the President."

"You his assistant or something?" Taking a bite of the McGriddle, barbecue sauce dripped from her plump lips.

"Comms," he said.

She shrugged, then looked around conspiratorially and leaned in. "Can you pass a message for me?"

Jay knew he wouldn't but wanted to hear what she had to say anyway. "Sure."

"I need you to DM my Instagram. I have an assistant running it. Sasha. No, wait, *fuck* Sasha." She seemed confused, somewhat delirious. "Tell whatever assistant is running it to send me some toner. I can't go on TV like this."

Jay was stunned. "You know you're being executed in a few hours, right?"

She waved her hand dismissively. "Yeah, right," she laughed. "Willem Loots assured me that I'm getting out of here."

"Willem Loots, huh?" Jay said.

"He's going to save this country from people like you," she said, shoving fries into her mouth. "Plus, I'm Kim Kardashian. They can't kill me."

Jay grinned. *Oh, yes, we will. And we're not stopping there.*

Two

June 18, 2038 | Las Vegas, Nevada

The doctor did not like Sasha.

"This is the third time," he scrolled through a tablet, "that Maya Ivanov has needed emergency insulin in the last two months. Medicaid should allot enough insulin for Maya," the doctor scolded. "If not, her school should have some on hand. You shouldn't be in the ER this often if you're properly managing her illness."

"Well, Medicaid and the school don't," Sasha said, "So, do you suggest I let her die?"

"Maya shouldn't even need to monitor her insulin this way," he said, softening. "An artificial pancreas would manage insulin for her."

"How would that work?" Sasha asked. He got up and examined a wall of pamphlets and chose a purple one and handed it to Sasha. Its cover featured a happy child with her shirt rolled up to the bellybutton.

"An artificial pancreas to monitor her illness. It's a simple surgery. Outpatient."

Sasha perked up. "That sounds great. What do you need from me?"

"We can schedule the surgery immediately. All I need is the guardian's signature..."

Shit. "Maya's father isn't exactly... available."

The doctor raised an eyebrow. "Maya's not your daughter? And you aren't her legal guardian?" Sasha glumly shook her head in response. The doctor glared at her. She'd been skirting that topic. "Then who are you?"

"I'm her aunt. I just moved back from LA. I'm taking care of her until—" the doctor cut her off. He'd heard this spiel too often.

"I'm sorry, Ms. Ivanov, but the regulations are quite clear. I can't perform this surgery without signed consent from the child's legal guardian. Your only options are to get your brother's signature or find a more reliable source for insulin," he looked at her, then squinted his eyes in recognition. "Why do you look familiar?"

"Just that kind of face," Sasha said, hoping he would drop it.

"No," he tapped his finger on his Loots Tablet, thinking, then snapped his fingers. "Dog shit girl!"

"I also put her away for fraud and manslaughter," Sasha mumbled. The part of the show trial everybody forgot.

"You made little gift baskets of dog shit for people who pissed her off," he said, shaking his head and laughing. "I knew I recognized you from somewhere. God, and to think she's going to die today. Well, anyway." He placed a sample-size vial of insulin on the counter. "This is the last vial I can provide for you this month. My recommendation: Get that signature."

Easier said than done. The dog shit girl snatched the vial.

Maya texted continuously as Sasha drove her back to school. Sasha glanced at the machinery monitoring her ten-year-old niece, the bulky fanny pack that Maya did her best to bedazzle and make fashionable, but still sat heavy around her bony hips. Maya wanted to be a dancer.

"Why didn't Aunt Olga give you your insulin shot this morning?" Sasha asked again.

"She told me not to tell you," responded Maya, without looking up.

"Well, I'm telling you *to* tell me, and I out-rank Aunt Olga because I bought you your iPhone."

Maya let out a long, performative sigh. "She sold it. She said it's rent day and we all have to pull our weight around here."

Sasha pounded the steering wheel with a fist. "What is wrong with her? The fucking bitch."

"Language!" Maya gasped, pretending to be shocked at the language she surely heard on the schoolyard every day.

Sasha pulled up outside of Maya's school and pulled over.

"In debate we're talking about Kim K Death Day," Maya said. "You're, like, a source. I'm arguing pro. Anything you want to add?"

Nothing about fecal matter. "There's video of her admitting to the Stockton poison leak and laughing at pictures of 'ugly' dead babies. You don't get more guilty than that."

"And you took that?" Maya asked.

"Sure did," she said. It was an assistant's job to be invisible. Sasha was good at it.

"Wow," Maya mulled it over in her head. "That's brave." Sasha smiled. She wasn't so sure anymore but ruffled Maya's hair anyway.

"You know, the doctor said you could get a surgery," Sasha said. "They'd insert something that would do it all for you. An artificial pancreas. You could live a normal life, he said."

Maya froze. "No more shots?" she asked hopefully.

Sasha nodded. "No more shots."

Maya's face brightened. "No more monitor?" she asked.

"I guess not," Sasha replied.

Maya beamed. "When can I do it?" she asked, practically bouncing in her seat.

Sasha took a deep breath. "We need your dad's signature."

Maya's face fell. "Oh." Even after completely disappearing from her life months ago, Dima still had the potential to disappoint his beautiful daughter. "See you later," Maya slammed the car door.

Sasha watched Maya walk up to school, her head hanging with the same weight as the monitor around her waist. She knew that she would do anything for that girl, go to any length she could to make a better life for her.

Dima was on top of diabetes in a good year. This was not a good year. The last time Sasha spoke to her brother was six months ago at the Einstein Bros. Bagels on Maryland Parkway. He was very thin, his head shrunken on top of his tall frame and broad shoulders. He kept insisting he was doing great, feeling healthy, really connected to the universe. Then he asked Sasha to Venmo him twenty dollars. He poured six packets of sugar into his coffee. He said he'd been speaking with demons.

"You just said you were doing well," Sasha said.

Dima shrugged. "I am. They're not so bad."

"What do they say?"

"They never shut up," he replied and laughed. He said Suboxone made him draw snakes and that hell exists in all our bodies near our lower intestines.

"Are you coming home any time soon?" she asked. Dima left for court mandated rehab when the cops picked him up on a disorderly nodding out at a slot at the El Cortez. Then, he never came back after the 30 days were up. He disappeared into the innards of the city, the tunnels that formed the foundation of the Strip. At the time, Sasha undertook a full-fledged manhunt for him. She put up flyers, organized search parties, even asked her pizza delivery clients if they had seen him. He was her brother, and even though he was a junkie, this is what people did for family.

"You need to take down the flyers," he said. "I'm not coming home."

"What about Maya?" He fidgeted, scratched the inside of his wrist. Sasha thought this shit was over. Dima had been on a four year stretch of "good dad" shit. He was a carpenter at the Convention Center. A union guy. He made weird chairs and sold them on the internet. He took Maya to museums and taught her how to draw.

"Maya is better off without me." He fixed his eyes on a spot near the soda fountain and his eyes narrowed. The demons.

Sasha did a bump of cocaine and drank two White Claws on the walk to Greg and Andrea's. Kim K Death Day required libations.

"Hey," Andrea said on Sasha's arrival, hugging her warmly. She was a mom, and, to Sasha, the platonic ideal of what a mom should be. Sasha's own mother was a human resources lawyer in Reno who defended the wrong side of sexual harassment cases and lost most of her earnings at keno. When Sasha told her that her only son was missing, her mother rolled her eyes over Face-Time and said: Again? He'll turn up.

Andrea always offered Sasha cocktails and a home-cooked meal and didn't care if she blacked out and slept on the couch. That's true love. Especially considering that when Sasha left after high school, she'd tried to put her Vegas life, and friends, behind her. The fact that Andrea and her husband Greg welcomed her back with kindness was one of the only good things about Sasha's life recently.

Greg set French appetizers out on the table. He admired his own cooking. "I thought French food may be fitting for the occasion," he said.

"Let them eat cake," Sasha said, and picked up an iced pastry and popped it into her mouth.

"Or dog shit," Greg said. Sasha groaned while everybody else laughed. Greg patted her on the shoulder. "Don't worry, as our whistleblower queen, you get a special whistleblower cocktail," Greg handed her a green cocktail with a little pink umbrella. "Tequila, chili pepper, lime, and agave for our Kardashian associate turned comrade in arms."

They all clinked glasses and then the subject was dropped for the duration of the evening. This was the only place Sasha would be able to feel comfortable for this event, considering her personal history with the person being executed. Anywhere else, she'd have to field weird questions or be asked to pose for selfies with people who recognized her from the show trial as the dog shit girl.

Sasha pitched the idea once as a joke.

Kim loved that kind of potty humor. She sent an edible arrangement of shit to her sister on the show. The stunt earned Sasha a producer credit. Then, Kim started doing it to executives and VPs she considered disloyal, who put in their notice or otherwise pissed her off. The more shit Kim got into, the more shit Sasha delivered. During Sasha's cross-examination at the trial, Kim whispered to her lawyers, winked at Sasha on the stand, and then the lawyer asked: "Did you add dog feces to an edible arrangement Ms. Kardashian sent to a close colleague?" A yes or no question that lacked the required context. Sasha guiltily stammered out a "Yes."

The press went wild. The moment was clipped everywhere. Suddenly, she wasn't a whistleblower. She was the dog shit girl. There went her book deals, her appearances on cable news. She slid back into obscurity. Nobody even asked her to comment on the execution.

Kim's final revenge.

"How are you?" Matt asked. Matt was her brother's best friend growing up. He had gotten clean. He fiddled with a Juul in his hand. Stick-and-poke tattoos dotted his arms and hands. His thick black hair was streaked with premature gray, unwashed and mussed around his head and he wore used military fatigues. It was a self-conscious and, if Sasha was being honest, kind of an embarrassing look he had curated as a part of his main source of income: a lefty podcast called "Deep Gate" about CIA conspiracies and associated Twitch stream where he played spreadsheet games about World War I for Venmo donations. He was part of the new communist vanguard busking for internet strangers to buy him a new gaming PC.

"Maya needs an artificial pancreas," Sasha said. "The insulin shortage fucked us. This is some AI organ that will create insulin for her. The pamphlet says it's $8,000. No Medicare for Kids coverage."

"Shit," Matt said.

"And I need Dima's signature," Sasha said, "Have you heard from him in, oh, the last six months?" Greg handed her a flute of champagne, and she produced a bag of ketamine from her back pocket. She began to arrange it in lines on the coffee table. She focused on ensuring the lines were even, fat, even though they were just for her.

"Not a word," said Matt. "You know how it is with him. I think he's pissed at me for something. Probably something to do with the demons." Sasha nodded in resignation.

On the flatscreen, a countdown clock ticked downward to the moment of the execution. The broadcast had the vibe of the Oscars pre-show. The host of the countdown, Mila Hager, George W. Bush's granddaughter, wore a designer black dress, had a beautifully blown-out blonde head of hair and Botox that Sasha thought was quite tastefully done. She smiled at the camera, her bleached white teeth beaming. "The countdown continues to tick down as more attendees arrive. After this quick break, we'll be right back with the execution of Kim Kardashian. Don't go anywhere."

An ad break before the public hanging. Only in America. Sasha huffed a snootful of K as the commercial panned in on a desert vista.

"Transport yourself from Nevada to a galaxy far, far away," an announcer's voice boomed from the flatscreen, over shots of middle-aged nerds driving land speeders across a salt flat. "Experience a weekend at Disney-Warner's Real Tatooine." A shot of men with toy lightsabers brutally attacking costumed actors dressed like Bedouin tribespeople.

"Oh good, our generation can take part in the most dangerous game," Sasha said.

Matt laughed, Greg seemed a little hurt. "I think it seems kind of cool," he said. "It looks super immersive. I want to go."

"We'll go, sweetie," Andrea comforted, touching his arm. "Ignore Sasha, she doesn't like anything."

Sasha rolled her eyes and turned back to the TV. "Real Tatooine, only in the Innovation Zone." The Nevada town of Pahrump had recently been unincorporated and re-formed as the nation's first Innovation Zone, a special district where corporations could technically exist as their own fiefdoms. Nevada, already basically lawless, had established a carved-out section where laws existed even less. It was a boon to corporations and to libertarian billionaires who had no intention of paying for the Communist President's hand-outs. Matt regularly ranted about the Innovation Zone on Deep Gate, but to Sasha it didn't seem different from how Nevada had always been. She was just annoyed that since its formation, TV ad breaks were blanketed wall-to-wall with local ads trying to entice people away from the Strip and into the Innovation Zone.

Sasha snorted a key bump from a small baggie of cocaine as the ad break rolled into an image of a sunrise over a town square lined with giant LED screens. A voice, too nasal and too stilted to be a professional voice actor, played over the images. "We're building something here. Something new. Something modern." The video cut to an image of a doughy haircut in an expensive suit and a tie patterned with cat memes standing on a high-rise balcony, desert sprawling behind him. "Something epic," he said with a crooked grin. A robot behind him winked at the camera.

"Boooo!" Matt shouted at the screen.

"America forgot how to build," the narration continued.

"What? You have a problem with Willem Loots?" Andrea screwed up her face at Matt.

"You don't?" Matt shot back. "He's the richest man in the world!"

"But we haven't," Loots continued as the video faded to a young professional working on a laptop in a serene open-plan office.

"He made that money from electric cars," Andrea retorted. "You're not against electric cars, are you?"

"He made that money from USwap, taking a vig on the transaction fee anytime someone sold their useless plastic trash,"

Matt said. "Besides, every car company makes electric cars now. Loots just makes self-driving ones that run people over."

Sasha grimaced and took a deep swig from her White Claw. Everyone had strong opinions on Willem Loots. Hers was unique—she didn't give a shit.

"Come build with us," Loots said from the TV as the ad faded to a group of smiling workers outside a collection of yurts. Sasha blinked hard. She wasn't sure if she believed her eyes.

"I hope Lopez does him next," said Matt.

"Oh, come on, now you're just being contrarian!" Andrea threw her hands in the air in exasperation.

"Rewind it for a second," said Sasha.

"What?" asked Greg.

Sasha grabbed for the remote, rewound to the group shot outside of the yurts and paused. "Hey!" a partygoer exclaimed. "I don't want to miss the execution," said another.

Sasha approached the TV and snapped a picture of the freeze-frame with her phone. She plopped back in her seat and zoomed in. She had to be sure of what she'd seen.

Her eyes had not deceived her. Pixelated though the image, there he was, with a wide smile across his face in the middle of the group.

It was Dima. On television. In Loots Town.

Greg reclaimed the remote and fast-forwarded to the live broadcast. President Lopez stood at a podium with a stern expression on his face, his speech already in progress. "Even when a trove of documents surfaced with her actual signature proving beyond a doubt that she was responsible for these decisions, what happened? The Democratic-Republican DOJ let her off with a slap on the wrist. She didn't serve a day of jail time. She paid a fine. For someone with the wealth of Kim Kardashian, it was like paying for a parking meter. Ms. Kardashian was directly responsible for the deaths of thousands, for the ruin of a working-class American town for perhaps generations to come, and yet she walked as a Free. Woman." He pointed his finger in the air, punctuating the last two words.

Matt's eyes were glued to the address from the President he

admired and had worked so hard to elect. Sasha nudged his shoulder and handed him her phone. Annoyance flashed across his face, he lowered his black-rimmed glasses and squinted. Then turned to Sasha wide-eyed. "Holy shit." His reaction confirmed to Sasha that it wasn't just the drugs and alcohol playing tricks on her. It was Dima. She nodded and took her phone back from Matt.

"Let this serve as a warning to those who would put profit over the lives and wellbeing of everyday Americans," Lopez continued, winding down his speech. "And may God bless the United States of America."

Lopez stepped from behind the podium and solemnly walked from the raised stage. The National Anthem started playing, and dramatic lighting lit up the stage. U.S. marshals walked Kim on stage. She wore a couture dress that Sasha remembered from a Met Gala seven years ago. She helped write a press release with a picture packet and video content from the fitting. The bodice was glittery and the sleeves ballooned out a foot or so from her shoulders, making her look like a cartoon villain. Even though her hair was blown out and her make-up was perfect, it was clear she had been roughing it. The make-up couldn't completely erase the acne. Weight gain had made her plastic surgery sit poorly on her face, weird and lumpy, like a Dune character. Baron Kim Harkonnen. Someone gasped.

"Look what they did to her big naturals!"

"We're gonna tell our children about the day Kim Kardashian was executed," Greg said, breathlessly. The camera panned in on the crowd in the Rose Garden. It was all people from the factory town. Some were clearly on chemotherapy, oxygen tubes coming out of their noses with bald heads or head scarves. A child near Maya's age stood alone near the back, gripping an IV. In a hushed tone, Mila explained that the girl's parents were dead. One from poor factory conditions, the other a few weeks later from suicide.

"Why bring a kid to an execution?" Andrea said. She looked over at the closed door by the kitchen where her toddler, Elliott, slept soundly.

"It's a show," Matt said, "I produce them every week."

Kim was flanked by guards with nightsticks. She stared straight ahead and smiled. She touched her hair and smoothed it down.

The vibe in the room had changed. People began to squirm, down their drinks. It was strange to watch this woman, clearly driven mad by prison, die on television.

A picture-in-picture box faded in on screen with live video of a crowd of protesters sobbing in pink "Save Kim" t-shirts. Another box appeared with a different crowd cheering, wearing "Kill the Rich" gear.

Kim continued to preen.

"Do you think the President will stop it at the last minute?" Sasha asked, measuring out a line with her debit card. "Casino odds are fluctuating."

"He's setting an example," Matt said. "The 1% were blatantly ignoring his new laws. They're not going to now."

"I hope he pardons her," a girl from high school whose name Sasha couldn't remember said. "I just hate the death penalty! So inhumane!" Sasha snorted another line.

Finally, the guards pushed Kim towards the gallows. She looked around and her eyes widened.

"No, wait. No," Kim said. Her eyes filled with panic. The guards tightened their hold on her. "This wasn't supposed to happen." She started to struggle against them wildly. Another guard seized her. "I'm Kim Kardashian!" she screamed. "You can't kill me. You love me! You all love me!" She struggled harder and in doing so, she hit one of the guards in the face. Blood streamed from his nose. Another guard pulled out a syringe and injected her with something that made her muscles immediately go slack.

"You love me," she said dreamily, and then slumped against the guards with a dull look.

"I wish I could get my hands on that drug," Sasha said as they put the noose (Union made!) around Kim's neck. Her eyes were dull and lifeless when the floor beneath her dropped. Sasha could hear the pop of her neck snapping. She hung there, swaying in the breeze, her body twitching a little bit, and then the broadcast faded to a slowly rippling American flag.

Matt turned to Sasha, a wide smile on his face. "How do you feel?"

"What do you mean?"

"I mean, you did this. If not for you, this might not have happened," Matt explained, with glee. If it were up to him, every person above his tax bracket would be in a noose. "So how does it feel?"

Sasha didn't feel anything at all.

Three

June 19, 2038 | Санкт-Петербург, Россия

Chloe Thibodeaux stood on the balcony of the Admiralteysky District apartment, her fake tan incongruous against the typically gray Russian sky. She squinted into the sun that peeked from behind the Lakhta Center, the shimmering skyscraper like a knife plunged from beneath the ground into the sky above. She thought of plunging a knife of her own as she twisted and toyed with the ends of her platinum blonde hair. It was a nervous tic, a bad habit holdover from her teenage years that she knew would hurt and fray the ends of her perfect hair.

Normally, her looks were everything. Normally, as an influencer, she would do anything to preserve them.

Today, she didn't care. In one night, she had lost everything. Now, the only thing she cared about was revenge.

He had taken everything from her.

He had to pay.

The Communist President Lopez had to die.

Eight hours earlier, Chloe had been in the mood to celebrate. It was nearing 4 AM (9 PM in Washington, D.C.), the scheduled time of the execution of Kim Kardashian.

Chloe had carefully moderated the amount of vodka she drank to ensure that she wouldn't fall asleep before the big event. It wasn't easy—the vodka was one of the only benefits of her new life in exile in frigid, gray Russia. Distilled by some Russian peasant by-hand, bottled, and delivered by-hand to her apartment. That was true craftsmanship, not Tito's made by some robot in New Braunfels fucking Texas. Real human blood and sweat and tears were in this vodka, hold the corn syrup. Who would trust someone named Tito to make vodka?

She had to take her pleasures where she could, because otherwise life in Russia was wretched. The schizophrenic weather, the decrepit buildings, the pallid paper-white skin on everyone. Chloe thought some of the women could potentially be hot if they had ever heard of Vitamin D. It was depressing.

Thankfully, despite her exile, despite her new life with the Oligarch who sponsored her existence, despite her days spent in the drafty apartment once owned by a count who killed himself and his family during one of Russia's boring revolutions, she still had a lifeline to a world where she mattered. 5,000 miles from a home she wasn't sure she'd ever be able to return to, she still had people who hung off her every word, who worshipped her like the icon she knew she was, who idolized her perfect skin, her perky tits, her tight body.

She still had social media.

Even with her slumlord ex Hunter awaiting trial in Guantanamo Bay, even with her own legal status in America questionable, her socials were a tether to her old life. With these valuable accounts, she didn't need a man like Hunter or the Oligarch to provide, she had managed to hang on to her value as an influencer with no more than her body. Hunter was the bad guy. She was collateral. Hot collateral.

Chloe live-tweeted along with the Russia Today broadcast of the execution festivities, President Lopez's speech was breathlessly re-translated into Russian on the flatscreen TV, its modernity out of place amidst the ancient apartment's opulent tapestries covering crumbling green walls and gilding. Seated in an overlarge chair with frayed upholstery was the apartment's only other resident, Sessa. The harsh Russian woman was a maid, presumably, but she had the stench of intelligence on her. She was always watching Chloe, her small brown eyes trained on her at all times, her hair always in a tight bun, her clothes always dark and drab.

Sessa pretended to be above the execution, as a Russian woman she pretended to be above everything, apathy as a world view, but Chloe caught her glancing up from the copy of *Anna Karenina* in her lap to look at the TV.

Chloe secreted a photo of Sessa with her phone and tweeted it out with a caption:

chloexoxox: Even my bitch Russian maid can't help but watch the show LOL #KimKDeathDay

Chloe caught moments of Lopez's speech as he paraded victims on stage: "We're doing this for our children. Tatia recently gave birth to a stillborn child after drinking arsenic-laced tap water due to pollution from the Kim Kardashian Beauty Plant in Stockton, California. These stories are not new to us. We've all heard them. They've happened to us."

Chloe respected that he had a good comms person. Nobody could ignore people who could be their neighbors looking totally fucked up.

The bloodthirsty President looked solemn as he stepped away from the lectern. The stage was bathed in gaudy, colorful lighting as the feed faded to a bunch of uniformed soldiers playing an ugly-sounding brass band rendition of the National Anthem.

Chloe was composing a tweet about how out of shape the soldiers looked when her phone buzzed. It was her manager LJ.

LJ: What's up, mama?

Chloe hated when LJ called her mama, despite the fact that she did have two children. Mama meant fat, the opposite of hot, the slippery slope to old.

LJ: Love the livetweet, babe.

Babe was better than Mama.

LJ: You've got us all busting up over here at the watch party!

Chloe sent a winking emoji.

LJ: O.M.G., you've got to see these!

LJ sent a picture of a platter of cupcakes adorned with a toy of Kim's head with Xs over the eyes.

LJ: Dead velvet cupcakes.

Chloe: Oh my god. STOP.

LJ: Soooo wish you were here, Mama.

Mama again. Ugh.

LJ: Go hard on Kim tonight. Hating the rich is in, and you're in a unique place as an influencer to hit her hard. You've got that authenticity that connects after everything that happened with Hunter. Really put the screws to her.

Chloe: You got it, babe.

LJ: Have fun with it! But don't have too much fun tonight, remember we've got the call with the Israelis tomorrow, bright and early your time.

Chloe was in final negotiations for a major sponsorship deal to be the brand ambassador for an Israeli skincare company. The lucrative deal was set to be finalized with a Zoom call in just a few hours. Goodbye Russia, hello Mediterranean!

On the TV screen, the moment of truth had finally arrived. Kim K made her appearance and Chloe noted with glee that she looked positively obese.

chloexoxox: wow looks like that was SOME last meal #KimKDeathDay

Then they killed her. They really did it.

The broadcast cut to Russia Today anchors, gleefully talking about how awesome America was. Fucking insane.

Chloe was struck with a burst of inspiration.

Chloe stood on one of the ancient upholstered chairs, wearing some oversized pajamas stuffed with pillows underneath. It was hilarious to make herself look fat, since her followers would know how far it was from the truth. She drafted Sessa's assistance, and the maid stood stone-faced holding a phone camera pointed at Chloe. The phone played audio of Kim's final words and Chloe mouthed along with them in an over-the-top pantomime.

"You can't kill me. You love me! You all love me!" Chloe mouthed along, rolling her eyes crazily and sputtering spittle. "You love me," she concluded. Then she pulled a makeshift noose constructed from scarves from behind her back and quickly threw it around her neck, then jumped from the chair to the floor, jerking her limbs around in a drag show parody of Kim's final breath. She rolled her head to her shoulder and lolled her tongue out of her mouth.

She snapped out of the performance, turning to Sessa. "Did you get it?"

Sessa shrugged. "I have no idea."

Chloe snatched the phone from her hand and watched the looping replay in the TikTok app. She squealed with laughter. It was hilarious. She looked just like fat-ass execution Kim and had lip synced her final words with perfection. She put a song over it. The song they played when Paul Walker kicked the bucket during the Fast & Furious movies. She played and re-played the loop. It was perfect. She checked the time, quickly calculating the time difference. 5 AM meant it was 10 PM on the east coast and 7 PM on the west coast. Perfect timing for this TikTok to do numbers.

She was sure it would do numbers.

She tapped out a quick caption saying she was surprised the noose didn't snap due to Kim's fat ass and accompanying it with the appropriate hashtags to get traction, and then hit post. It sailed out into the world, and reactions immediately began rolling in. The rolling laughing emoji. Comments reading "LMFAO." She was good at what she did. And her people loved her for it. In the morning, she'd be paid lavishly for it.

Maybe life in exile wasn't so bad.

She settled back into a too-large chair, poured herself a tall glass of celebratory peasant blood vodka, and was lulled to sleep by the reactions from her adoring public back home.

In her dream she went back to the day it happened again. She was naked, doing yoga on the deck of their old home in Carmel-by-the-Sea, looking at the Pacific Ocean in Warrior II pose, relishing the feeling of sweat pouring into rivulets formed by the protruding rib bones between her tits, knowing it was making her body thin and beautiful. Knowing her body was all she had, that she was getting older and that, for a woman like her, older meant death. She was 35 and she had no idea what to do besides contort her body into weird positions and rub it with lotion and inject it with various chemicals to keep it 30. Always 30.

A SWAT team entered the compound. She heard them rustle through the brush and hastily put a robe on her naked body as they swarmed the house with guns and flashlights. Turning everything over. Confiscating hard drives. Tearing the stuffing from furniture looking for more.

The fear in Hunter's face as they forced him into handcuffs. The unattractive desperation as he called out to her. "Wait for me!"

She knew what happened next, she'd lived it a thousand times since that day at Carmel-by-the-Sea. They'd pummel Hunter, put him in handcuffs, and stuff him in the back of a squad car, the first steps on his journey to a cell in Guantanamo awaiting prosecution for his crimes under the Free America Act.

But, tonight, it didn't happen.

She stood on the front porch, the salty sea air blowing her robe open, as she stared out at a gallows on the front lawn that, in the dream, had always been there.

Hunter was fat now, like Kim, in an orange jumpsuit, looking like a spray-tanned Saddam Hussein with rat's nest hair and a graying five o'clock shadow. The SWAT team marched him up the stairs of the gallows and fitted the noose around his neck. He looked her directly in the eyes.

"You love me," he gasped.

"I don't," she replied. She never had. The trap door swung open beneath his feet and the rope choked the life out of him.

She woke with a start as Sessa slammed a book on a table. Normally she'd be annoyed at Sessa's passive-aggressive fake-cleaning which so often involved waking her from vodka slumbers, but today she was more concerned about being awake in time for her important Zoom with the Israelis. She checked the time on her phone —it was 7 AM. She still had an hour to shower and freshen up to look her best on the video call. She tapped to TikTok to get another gratifying hit of mention-dopamine, but the app spat out an error and wouldn't load. The fucking thing was always crapping out since the Chinese had been forced to sell it to Aetna.

Fuck it. She headed to the bathroom to start the long process of running the shower so it would be slightly warmer than ice cold. When Chloe arrived, Sessa said it was better to boil water and pour it into a plastic bucket and do a grown-up sponge bath. This country couldn't do anything right.

She had only moments to spare after showering, blowing out her hair, and carefully applying makeup. She angled her laptop to catch the Saint Petersburg skyline outside the balcony behind her and connected to the Zoom call.

LJ appeared in a small box. "Hey, Mama." She had a sour look on her face. Probably hungover, Chloe noted with annoyance. Real good, LJ, after her scolding about not having too much fun last night. She made a mental note to seek new representation as soon as this deal went through.

Another square appeared with Hebrew lettering. Kfir Peretz sat at his desk in Tel Aviv. She could see the warm Mediterranean glittering behind him, and it made her a little wet to see the ocean and the sun. The real sun, not the Scandinavian imposter outside her window. She smiled broadly but it faded when she saw the look on Kfir's face. Grim, his mouth set, his eyes boring a hole into her MacBook Pro.

"Hello ladies, and thank you for your time today," he said in perfect, accented English.

"Thanks, babe, how's Tel Aviv? It looks beautiful!" Chloe always started meetings with inane small talk. He didn't take the bait.

"I suppose you've checked the American news this morning," he said. Chloe flicked her eyes over to LJ, who quickly looked down at her phone.

"No," Chloe said apprehensively. "Late night, with the Kim thing and all," she added with a smile.

Kfir groaned, muttering a few words in Hebrew, then put a link in the chat. Chloe clicked and swallowed at the headline. They only used her married name when it was a hit piece.

CHLOE MEADOWS DEMONETIZED AND BANNED FOR KIM KARDASHIAN HATE SPEECH

Chloe Meadows, now Thibodeaux, wife of disgraced billionaire Hunter Meadows, was permanently suspended from Aetna Inc.'s TikTok after a late-night post about the late Kim Kardashian. The video has been permanently deleted but the Post has reviewed a copy. Meadows-Thibodeaux re-enacted and mocked the final moments of Ms. Kardashian's life.

Experts believe it was in violation of the 2036 Social Media Regulation Act barring all hate speech on social media platforms. Under the act, signed into law by President Lopez during his first hundred days in office, social media platforms are liable for user content but are additionally able to sue users for violating their terms of service. TikTok's parent company Aetna Inc. would not specifically comment on whether they are pursuing litigation against Meadows-Thibodeaux, only saying in a statement "For now, her accounts are suspended and demonetized."

Disney-Warner's Twitter and Berkshire Hathaway's Meta quickly followed suit, disabling Meadows-Thibodeaux's accounts on those platforms. Meadows-Thibodeaux's sponsors, including Australian pharmaceutical company SOLARVAC, are pulling their contracts.

"SOLARVAC is about simplifying nutrition, not encouraging violence, even against condemned criminals." Kardashian's 83-year-old mother, Kris Jenner, had this to say on Twitter: "Horrible news. Really. Kim was nothing but nice to Chloe Meadows. Nothing but nice to anybody. If SOLARVAC or anyone else is looking for a new sponsor, my daughter Kylie is available and KIND!"

The White House released a statement from Chief of Staff Lupe Fox, widely known to be a key early booster of the Social Media Regulation Act. "This is just another example of our administration holding the wealthy accountable and why I hope this Congress will support legislation to expand the Social Media Regulation Act. As we have said time and time again, posts like this one from Chloe Meadows are literally violence."

This story is developing. The Post reached out to Meadows for comment, but her representatives did not respond in time for publication.

Bullshit. She had no emails from the Post in her inbox.

The Zoom call didn't last much longer. Kfir calmly informed Chloe that his company obviously couldn't do business with her anymore and would be pulling the contract. He ended the call before Chloe could even make her case.

After the call, LJ sent Chloe a text – a TEXT – dropping her as a client. Chloe frantically texted back that she could get back on socials, that she had contacts in American tech. The texts just showed an insulting read receipt. No reply came.

So, Chloe stood on the balcony, staring at the Lakhta Center and imagining plunging it into the Communist President's chest. She was stuck. Stuck with Sessa and with the Oligarch and his inane weekly dinners where he just stared, wondering what to do with her.

The Communist President should thank her. This was all free promo for his agenda. Yet here she was.

Her phone buzzed. It was a notification from an encrypted message app, from the person whose contact she'd saved in her phone as Rocket-Emoji Man. Willem Loots. She was proud to have gotten very close to an affair with the controversial billionaire during an MDMA-heavy night in his parked private jet at Burning Man.

She swiped open the app, lonely and desperate for any kind of acknowledgment that she existed from anyone who mattered. She saw two messages:

rocketman69💩💩: saw what happened w u. sux.

rocketman69💩💩: someone needs to do something about the pinko pres

She furiously typed a response: Someone should kill him.

She stared at the phone intently as the three "typing" bubbles appeared from Loots. He typed for a little too long, she worried that in her anger she had gone too far, turned him off.

Finally, a reply appeared. Loots sent the thinking-face emoji.

Four

June 27, 2038 | Pahrump Valley, Nevada

The 6.1-mile-long racetrack at Spring Mountain Motor Resort and Country Club was surrounded by condos, a clubhouse, and a wraparound lazy river. The lettering denoting the convention center was falling off. The place was never overflowing with guests.

To the mercenaries, it looked abandoned.

Dust kicked up in billowing clouds in the flat desert surrounding the club. ATVs sped by maneuvering around sagebrush and gullies. The drivers were a collection of private security and former police officers, amped up on adrenaline and amphetamines.

They came to a stop and moved under the cover of the moonless night towards the chain-link fence that surrounded the complex. The leader cut the fence and motioned for the men to come through and fan out, assault weapons drawn. They moved silently, a spear tip breaching the edges of Loots Town. The glowing tower provided the only light in the sky.

A cabana bar rotted and sagged inwards rimming a cracked pool. A pair of crows watched them infiltrate the area quietly. A mercenary, who two years prior was parking enforcement, took in the stagnant pool water carpeted with algae beside the cracked racetrack.

"Weird fucking place," she murmured, and the squad leader immediately shushed her.

A loud bang made the mercenaries duck behind overturned lounge chairs. State-of-the-art flares hovered in the night sky, blinding the mercenaries, and lighting the pool area, exposing their position. The team heard explosions and the whir of helicopters approaching.

A drug dealer fired a grenade launcher directly into the air as bullets strafed him and he fell backwards. The grenade fell twenty yards from the mercenaries and the force of the explosion threw them backwards with extraordinary force. A highly trained group of soldiers made a circle around the disoriented team as the flares burned out.

The mission was compromised. The team captain hurled his orders to retreat before getting hit with a volley of bullets. Blood spurted from his mouth as he fell to the ground.

Amped up and scared with assault rifles already in hand, their leader dead, and not knowing what to do, the mercenaries did what felt natural—they fired indiscriminately. Three of the group were floored by friendly fire. The rest fired outward with a deafening staccato.

A whistle screamed through the air. Cluster munitions lit up the sky so that the members of the team could see each other in brilliant, white light before fire rained down on them and the ground shook.

When the dust cleared, a soldier from the balcony of what was once a convention center flicked a cigarette onto the charred remains of the team.

"Don't fuck with Loots Town," he said.

FIVE

June 29, 2038 | Washington D.C.

"It all started with a reply to one of your tweets." Jay tapped the remote in one of the myriad identical conference rooms in the West Wing. The presentation transitioned to a screenshot of a tweet from Pablo. "'When I win the presidency, the rich are finally going to pay their fair share... with interest,'" Jay read.

"I wrote that?" Pablo asked, his feet kicked up on the desk. "Not bad."

"*I* wrote that, actually, but that's beside the point." Jay clicked to the next slide. "Billionaire Willem Loots replied, and I quote, 'brb seceding from the United States.' Everybody had a laugh. Another quirky tweet from the electric car guy. It turned out it wasn't a joke. A month later, Loots bought up fifty square miles of Pahrump Nevada and declared its independence from the greater United States. Loots Town. An actual law in Nevada, by the way. Corporations are allowed to form separate governments called, I shit you not, 'Innovation Zones.' So, yeah, legalized insurrection."

"Not that we don't appreciate your flair for the dramatic, Jay," Lupe said, tapping her pen on a blank notepad, "but the President has a lot on his schedule today. We all know the backstory. Get to the point." Lupe found his off-the-cuff presentation attitude distasteful, as she had written in many memos and long-texts to him over the past few years. As a Brown graduate, she did not like PowerPoints that weren't meticulously branded and rehearsed, accompanied by polling and data.

Jay shook her off. "The town quickly attracted thousands of terrified millionaires and tech bros, but Loots found out that his base had no ability to do any kind of real work at all. Quickly spin up a blog? These guys could do it. Operate a functional sanitation system? The people who lived in Loots Town were not up to the task. That's when Loots started recruiting the homeless."

"The unhoused," Lupe corrected.

"Yes, thank you, Lupe. Loots mounted a massive promotional campaign encouraging the *unhoused* from every major metropolitan area to relocate to Loots Town. Sounds great in theory. However, this was smuggled out of a Loots facility." Jay played a grainy video, taken furtively on an ancient cell phone of a warehouse with shit-stained cots, jammed with people shooting up and warming themselves by makeshift fires. "Loots denies this, of course. His town lies under a shroud of secrecy akin to North Korea. All we have is videos like this and the rare testimony from those who are allowed to leave." Jay played another video. Dozens of people digging ditches, repairing HVAC units, trimming hedges, and repairing roofs in the sweltering heat. "By the time they realized what they signed up for, that they weren't being paid or properly housed, they were stuck in a highly-militarized fiefdom."

Pablo raised an eyebrow but Jay couldn't tell if he was convinced or if he was just humoring him. Jay switched to the video footage from the other night of the downed mercenary team being riddled by bullets at an abandoned country club.

"Not to mention the massacre that occurred just this week. 12 men dead in the 'no man's land' just outside Loots Town. Loots's property, but outside the innovation zone. Those are cluster munitions, illegal under international treaty, being used against a flimsy force. I think if we launched a full congressional probe with the weight of the administration behind it, we would easily find that he is breaking dozens of federal laws under the Free America Act," Jay concluded.

Pablo sat at the end of the table with an eyebrow raised, considering. Lupe, as always, was laser-focused on his reaction so that she could immediately mirror it. "He seems like a real piece of shit," Pablo finally said.

"Right?" Jay replied excitedly.

Pablo planted his feet on the floor, leaned in and tapped his desk in thought. "I'm just not sure. Aren't those guys who got killed gig mercenaries? Nevada has stand your ground laws. And is that," Pablo squinted at the looping footage of the doomed mercenary team, "a grenade launcher?"

Lupe perked up. "Fact checkers at the Disinformation Bureau rated those videos as a 'big maybe.' Friends of mine at the NSA think it's Russian propaganda."

Jay rolled his eyes and appealed to Pablo. "Something is going on here. I know it."

"The innovation zones, while unfortunate, are a release valve for the public's reaction to change. It helps them cope *and* they are a bastion to sex workers from all over the country who need a safe haven. If we start screwing with them, people are going to be pissed." This was Lupe's greatest fear (and biggest kink, Jay theorized), that people would become mad, or mad at her, and she would need to go on Instagram Live in tears and call them names.

Pablo pondered on their arguments for a moment as Jay and Lupe stared, scrutinizing his reaction. Jay considered how odd it was to have a life where everything came down to one man's decision. "Jay," Pablo said finally, "this was a great presentation. And what's happening in Loots Town is alarming, to be sure." *Shit*, Jay thought. *He* was *humoring me*. "But I'm with Lupe on this. There's not enough evidence to make this a priority, and it's too much of a hot button issue this close to the midterms."

Lupe positively beamed.

"That's why I'm asking we find more evidence, not execute the guy in the town square," Jay said.

"But that's your ultimate goal, right?" Lupe said, tilting her head to the side.

"We took a lot of heat over the Kardashian execution," Pablo thoroughly rehashed Lupe's post-mortem on the execution. "It was popular at the time, but the post-execution polling showed a downtick in approval. I think it still came as a shock for a lot of Americans to watch an execution of such a persona on live TV. Willem Loots is almost as high-profile as Kim was. My feeling is: I think we made our point."

Jay's heart sank. Pablo reeked of the "conventional wisdom" they ran against, about slow, incremental change rubber-stamped by corporations. The type of politics that pushed America to the brink and demolished the two-party system. Putting the rich on trial wasn't about "making a point" for Jay, it never had been. It was about holding the wealthy accountable for once. For the *first time ever*.

"We need to show people that this administration isn't about bloodlust, it's about restoring the American Dream for everyone." Pablo leaned in, addressing Jay directly in that presidential way that made you feel special. "We can revisit this if anything new happens. For now, stand down. Last week, we showed the power of the Free America Act. Now, it's time to flex our muscle with other priorities." Pablo could read the disappointment on Jay's face. "You did great work, Jay. Thank you."

"*Such* great work," Lupe added, patronizing. Jay just glared at her, quietly furious.

This wasn't how it was supposed to go. The rich were supposed to go down. All of them.

Six

June 29, 2038 | Washington D.C.

Late into the night, Pablo thumbed through a deck of playing cards with pictures of nude women, which had been left in the office by Lyndon Johnson, and tried not to let his feelings play on his face, fearing that if some self-serving aide saw the look he would see it described in excruciating detail in a snarky Politico newsletter three hours from now.

Pablo let Jay down, and he couldn't tell him why.

That morning, Admiral Hantz came to see him. The wide shouldered sailor wore a dark navy suit with a coat and trousers. He was visibly uncomfortable in them despite his rigid posture. Pablo was not a fan of the U.S. military, but, despite that, always found himself somewhat tickled by servicemen. In a town where everyone was so coiffed and jacked-up with facial fillers to look their best well into their octogenarian years, servicemembers always looked so dumpy and out of place with their square jaws, pocked faces, and bad haircuts. They were like high school football coaches in a sea of Vanity Fair Oscars after-party attendees. Hantz entered the Oval with short, measured steps and shook Pablo's extended hand.

"Good to see you, Admiral," Pablo said. "But I have to warn you, you won't change my mind on increasing the military budget. Just don't want to waste your time." Pablo invited him to sit.

Hantz shook his head slightly, taking a seat on the opposite side of the Resolute. Pablo caught a hint of worry in the Admiral's eyes. These types were always so self-consciously stoic. "I'm afraid we're well past that point, Mr. President."

Pablo leaned against the desk with his arms folded. "Explain."

"Permission to speak freely, sir?"

Pablo nodded.

"The United States military is in a dire state, sir. My colleagues would ask you for more money to address it, but it's my opinion that our massive budget may be a source of the problem."

"Not the usual song and dance you people give me," Pablo said.

"Sir, our military is the most well-funded on the planet, but this has caused a culture of excess and waste that has put us in a worse and worse position. Trillions of dollars spent on the F-35s which still don't work. Administrative budgets with $2,109 line items for a single coffee cup. Billions on Hollywood movies. Fraud. Waste. Expensive and largely ineffective defense contracts," the Admiral straightened one of his many medals. "To be completely frank, our massive military budgets have served mostly to boost the stock prices of aerospace companies."

Pablo was astonished at his frankness. He'd heard like-minded lefties talk like this, read APP polemics with this tune, but military brass never talked like this.

"The Joint Chiefs won't tell you this," Hantz said. "They don't care about defending this country. They don't think it's at risk anymore. I asked for a private meeting because I do, and this is my last resort."

Pablo nodded his assent. Hantz briefed him on the state of the troops. They were soft. They hadn't won a war in nearly a century. They were better outfitted than at any point in history, but they barely knew how to use the unwieldy equipment. They were used to endless deployments on cushy islands, sitting in air-conditioned tents, playing video games. The Admiral believed with all seriousness that there would be a mutiny if there was an Xbox Live outage.

Hantz leaned forward, his eyes meeting Pablo's. "I know you're anti-war, Mr. President. I know that we don't see eye-to-eye on much, if anything. But I tell you this to help you understand the razor's edge that we find ourselves on. If the right adversary attacked us, on American soil, we would lose."

Pablo leaned back in his chair. He let the information sink in, swirl around his ideology, and settle into a deep fear. Jay was right about Loots, but there was nothing he could do to reign in someone with cluster munitions. He couldn't let the rich call the country's bluff.

Being the President sucked.

Seven

July 2, 2038 | Las Vegas, Nevada

The day was so hot that the concrete outside burned her feet.

"Alex the weed guy is *dead*?" Sasha exclaimed, smoking a cigarette by the over-chlorinated apartment pool. Maya had roped Sasha into being a lifeguard so she invited Matt over to keep her company while the girls played.

"MercGo contract," Matt said, sucking on his Juul. Despite living in the desert, his white skin was nearly translucent in the 110-degree heat. MercGo was corporate America's response to the largely defunded police forces. Anybody with a driver's license could be hired to provide "security" for events or, Sasha supposed, infiltrate Loots Town.

Sasha whistled. "Alex *would* be stupid enough to go head-to-head with Loots's army for a $270 app contract."

"Sasha," Maya yelled, jumping up and down in the water. "Latasha and Megan both want to be my best friend and I don't know what to do."

"Make them compete," Sasha yelled back, cracking open a tall boy, "May the best woman win!"

"Oh my God," she said, her eyes lighting up. "Great idea!" Latasha and Megan glared at Sasha from the pool as Maya started giving them detailed instructions.

Matt watched Sasha drink the beer. "Isn't it a bit early?"

"For what?" Sasha said. Her shift was over. She made a cool $57 minus gas delivering pizzas and liquor and Panda Express to drunk dentists at a conference downtown. Drinking at appropriate times meant you lived an appropriate life.

"Aren't you worried about Dima?" Matt said. "He's living with those trigger-happy assholes."

"I'm *worried* about finding a new weed guy." Coke and Ketamine too. Shit, it was nearly impossible to find decent drugs in Las Vegas, where the vast majority of customers were one-off tourists that usually bought Excedrin they thought was MDMA in the bathroom of Planet Hollywood.

"You're not afraid to go to Loots Town?" Matt asked.

"I don't plan on bringing a grenade launcher with me," Sasha said. The truth was, she'd exhausted all of her other options. Alex, may he rest in peace, had introduced her to a guy named "Foul Ball" who could get black market insulin but when Sasha arrived there were too many red flags, even for her. Meth, guns, heroin, tweakers. She'd read horror stories about people buying insulin that wasn't stored correctly and getting hospitalized. If whatever Foul Ball was peddling even was insulin—he didn't even have a refrigerator.

Then there was Denise. Even if she could track down Maya's mother, Denise had long ago signed away her rights to Maya for a couple grand. Maya was born premature. The doctor later told Dima that Maya nearly suffocated herself in the womb by somersaulting over her own umbilical cord. Fifteen minutes after Maya was lifted out of Denise's belly, Denise was in the bathroom shooting up fentanyl with her dealer. Suffice it to say, Denise checked herself out of the hospital early, leaving Maya with Dima. Permanently.

"This is for Kim, bitch!" The woman from 11A squirted a dollop of mayonnaise on Sasha's face from the third-floor balcony. Sasha grimaced and wiped the sauce off. It was already hot. 11A hoisted a bag of White Claws over her head in triumph and walked back into her apartment.

"Jesus," Matt said, "Does that happen often?"

It used to happen all the time, anytime she went out, when she did all those interviews on CNNBC, Good Morning America, and Vox. They saw Sasha as a threat to the American Dream. There was even a Reddit board dedicated to placing hexes on her for the good of womynkind.

"Alright," Sasha said, flicking her cigarette into the bushes. "Out of the pool, Maya." Maya and the girls groaned. They were in the middle of an underwater dance competition. "I have to go find your dad." Maya's eyes widened.

Matt wound the car through Henderson, up and around the Spring Mountains while Sasha did bumps of cocaine, drank steadily, and read Wikipedia. All the private land in Pahrump Valley was found in nine townships of six square miles of land, each in a desolate spat of desert between Death Valley and the Spring Mountains.

There had been high expectations for Pahrump when prospectors bombed and looted the Comstock Lode up north then sawed the tops off the muddy hills in Tonopah in search of silver and gold. People made plans for the region based on speculators and the nineteenth century version of fake news. When no fortune panned out, a religious group moved from Santa Ana, California to start a utopian desert colony outside of Earth's laws, a venture that resulted in six lines of vertical space in a newspaper and nothing else. They threatened to abandon the U.S. constitution in favor of God's, but nobody made good on their word and Pahrump went on existing as a remote weigh station between here and there until Las Vegas, booming and busting and busting, then someone thought: we ought to build a highway. Now there were six casinos and some retirees.

A true American story.

"President Lopez's next fight? Big Media. 'We stand behind the court's decision on Ms. Kardashian and are assured that the justice system will be tough on white collar crime. The White House is now focused on breaking up monopolies and making the American market competitive again,' Chief of Staff, Lupe Fox, told reporters during a press conference this morning.'"

Matt kept one eye on the dark road to Pahrump and the other on his cell phone where he changed podcasts schizophrenically every 90 seconds from politics, to news, to business: "The whistleblower, Sasha Ivanov, was a real wake-up call for entrepreneurs in North America. In order to scale, we need to think *globally*. Malaysia. Cambodia. Guatemala. The United States still has a wealthy class of people to consume our products but there is no longer a class to produce our products," a podcaster read out over ominous music punctuated by Israeli mattress commercials.

"Can you turn this off?" Sasha finally snapped. Matt turned down the volume.

"I don't know why you don't like talking about it," Matt said, "You're a hero."

"I'm not a hero," Sasha said, sighing. "I'm an idiot, a vain one too. At the time, people said I was helping my country. Saving people. I lapped it the fuck up. If I was smart, I would have blackmailed Kim. Gotten a nice payout to take care of Maya, Olga, my family. Bought them a house, good doctors. Then I wouldn't be here, driving to a place I may get killed to find my junkie brother. There is no good change. There is nothing we can do for our country. The people in power, whether they're socialist or Democratic-Republicans, they don't give a shit about us. They only care about their own asses. The only people we can help or trust with any certainty are our friends and family. Beyond that, we're fucking powerless."

"I think when people are more informed then things can get better," Matt said.

"That's cute of you, but the more informed people are, the more miserable they are," Sasha said, then leaned forward. "Holy shit." The Pahrump valley opened up on sandbags, neatly piled on top of each other. Old Gulf War era Humvees scattered along the road, presumably to scare anybody who dared enter. A tent city centered around an old ARGO gas station. Fires lit the town. Soldiers sat with machine guns in their laps, playing cards and checking their phones.

A soldier waved them into a checkpoint. Matt rolled down the window.

"ID, sir," the soldier said, spitting dip onto the side of the road. Matt opened his ID app and handed the man his phone. His eyes flicked from the phone to Matt's face and back. He sighed and then launched into a prepared speech: "Are you aware that you are leaving United States territory and entering a Nevada Innovation Zone. United States law is not enforced. If you dial 911, the local innovation zone authorities will be called. If you commit a crime, you are subject to local laws. If you need assistance, you are subject to local services. The United States has no jurisdiction there."

"Yes, Sir," Matt said.

"Alright, then," the guy said. He looked over at Sasha and winked. "Have fun."

---

10 miles of road separated the U.S. Army checkpoint and the innovation zones. Pahrump (now New Pahrump) was not what Sasha remembered from any previous excursions on the way to do acid or blow up fireworks on BLM land. The city itself was divided by lines of red and green. Red for Ft. Cathouse, the "innovation zone" of a Texas oil magnate. Women dressed in vintage lingerie blew kisses at the car while men open carried and drank rye whiskey on the streets of a rebuilt Western town square. People did wheelies on off road vehicles and raced each other down thoroughfares.

The green zone of Samhain was lined with magic shops, magic mushroom experiences, women breastfeeding children on the streets in white smocks, and cultivating gardens. A sign in green neon read: WE'RE HUMAN, NOT VACCINE from the old Golden Nugget, now a Healing Center where an impromptu drum circle gathered in the cracked parking lot. People raved with glow sticks and set off fireworks.

Finally, they hit black. Loots Town. Self-driving electric vehicles patrolled the perimeter, hitting curbs every now and then. As Matt and Sasha crossed the street, avoiding a Pegasus, a man ran forward and waved them down next to a World War II panzer tank dug halfway into the desert. The visitor's center. Great.

While Ft. Cathouse and Samhain welcomed guests, be it with whores or cottage core, Loots Town welcomed them with a barbed wire fence and a uniformed man packing a serious machine gun. A few workers in blue jumpsuits dug what looked like a moat separating Loots Town further from the other innovation zones. A skyscraper rose like a glass icepick.

"Name?" The armed man produced a tablet.

"Do we, uh, need reservations?" Matt asked. The guy looked up, annoyed, and shifted his body so a side-pistol faced Matt's face. Sasha cut in.

"I'm looking for my brother, Dmitry Ivanov." The guy scrolled through his iPad.

"Name?" he asked.

"Sasha Ivanov."

"What brings you to Loots Town?" He asked.

"To say hello?" Sasha said.

"One minute," The dude jogged over to the other side of the tank and radioed into town. He kept looking over at them as he talked to whoever else was on the line.

"I don't get it," Matt said, "The rest of the place is open. Why the secrecy?" Sasha shrugged as the guy jogged back.

"Dmitry Ivanov is out right now."

"Call him back and say it's about his fucking daughter," Sasha said.

"He's incommunicado. Even if he wasn't, it takes Loots Town 24 hours to process a visa."

"A *visa*?" Sasha asked. "Are you kidding me?"

"And just so you know we have a quarantine procedure for entry and exit that takes up to three days."

"I have to go to work tomorrow!" Sasha exclaimed. The soldier was unrelenting.

"Security is security, miss. You can transmit your ID info to me to process your visa and come back in the morning, or you can leave and never come back. It's up to you."

Sasha put the car in drive, intending to turn around when Matt stayed her hand. "Wait, I mean, maybe we should check it out?"

The Loots goon cleared his throat. "We don't process visas just for anyone, by the way. You're on Dmitry Ivanov's green list." Wow, a green list! Completely normal! Sasha was ready to go back and spange on the street for insulin if she had to.

"Think of Maya," Matt said. Sasha looked at the gate to Loots Town. A smokestack rose beyond the gate. Men worked across the perimeter putting up barriers and cameras, making it so she couldn't see anything.

Sasha sent her identification to the goon. As she did so, a rocket launched into the air with a sonic boom. It heaved itself up into the air before exploding above the mountains. She could hear the anti-vaxxers from Samhain oohing and aahing.

Eight

July 2, 2038 | Санкт-Петербург, Россия

It had been nearly two weeks since she had heard from Willem. Two weeks of pure isolation, not only in real life, but more importantly, online:

@savechloe2038: No one gives a SHIT what you think, Chrissy! PS: Weren't you telling teenagers to off themselves a couple decades ago??? Leave Chloe ALONE!

Chloe furiously drafted a Tweet from one of her many burner accounts, the iPhone clack sound effect and the tapping of her long fingernails effecting a double-staccato rhythm as she did. She tapped "SEND" and the app displayed a warning:

Health professionals have determined that some phrases used in your post may lead to illegal adverse mental health effects. Are you sure you want to send?

Without reading the entire warning, Chloe tapped "Yes" and the tweet soared out into Chrissy Teigen's mentions.

Chloe changed position in the uncomfortable, upholstered chair. She thought her new VPN and burners would help her work out some negative energy. And it did, but nobody paid attention to "Melissa from Wisconsin" the way they did to "Chloe Thibodeaux, lifestyle guru."

Attention was what she really craved, and she couldn't get the attention she needed as just another no-profile-pic nobody shrieking into the void of celebrity mentions. She was just another of the nothing people, part of the infinite scrum of non-participants bellowing jealous at the people who had made something of themselves. She had become that which she used to denounce almost daily, she realized with a shudder. A *hater*.

She hated this, the feeling of not having enough money and not knowing where she would get it next. It was overwhelming and all-encompassing, a thought loop from which it was impossible to break. It was like drowning—fighting against the currents to find a gasp of life-saving air only to be pulled right under again, taking a lungful of water. Only it was more like being waterboarded, Chloe thought, because some sick fuck was torturing her on purpose out of some twisted conception that it was somehow making his country better. How did the nothing people do this? How did they subject themselves to a never-ending cycle of drowning, of seeking a sense of relief that would never come? Chloe grew up in a trailer park with no father, a drunk mother, and too many siblings. She remembered her mother, bent over the sink, the fleshy trucker colliding with her over and over again in a forgotten Kentucky trailer.

Chloe would not go back to poverty.

A few days ago, Chloe made a desperate pass at the Oligarch. At the end of one of their sporadic lunches, she had sat herself on his lap and begun playfully toying with his chest hair. When she went to unbutton his shirt, he pushed her hand aside. With a soft chuckle (not at her expense, but, in that Russian way, at the absurdity of life itself), he told her gently that this was not the type of relationship they had. Seeing her disappointment, he brushed her hair off of her face and comforted her, telling her that everything would be alright. She believed him. She felt childlike, sitting in the lap of this man, larger than life but also physically large, like a barn, and she allowed herself to be comforted, just for a moment.

Sessa emerged (did she live in the apartment?) with a plate of pasta mixed with long stringy onions covered in oil and lit a cigarette. Chloe forced a fake cough, the American signal for "don't smoke around me" but that was a gesture that didn't translate into Russian, and Sessa just gave a Slavic stare that could either mean disdain or total disregard. Chloe considered going back inside, but she was so starved for attention she deigned to converse with Sessa.

"I'm fucked," she said, leaning on the balcony railing.

"Aren't we all?" Sessa responded with a nod.

"You don't understand. I've lost everything, and now I can't even work. They won't let me. The *Communist President* won't let me."

"When the Soviet Union collapsed, we had no work anywhere," Sessa responded, distant. She took a drag from her cigarette. "There was work to be *done*, of course, but no one was in charge of getting anyone to do it. So," she shrugged, "nobody worked."

Chloe hung off every word. It wasn't what she said so much as receiving attention at all. "So, what did you do?"

"Mostly, we boiled roots." Her lips upturned slightly. Was this a smile? "And drank."

As Chloe contemplated a carbohydrate-fueled future, her phone vibrated, and she snatched it off the chipped side-table thinking it was a Chrissy stan righteously fact-checking "Melissa" and insisting that Chrissy did nothing wrong. It's amazing how people thought the ineffectual act of typing a tweet built up virtue in their little good deed well.

It was Willem.

rocketman69💩💩 *:* sorry got caught up in some stupid shit. had to kill some mercenaries lol. didn't forget abt u.

Chloe held the phone to her chest and closed her eyes.

chloexox: i totally know the feeling. what's up?

It must be the middle of the night in America.

rocketman69💩💩 *:* I didn't forget what you said and I'm totally down to do it... I just need your help first. Check your email.

rocketman69💩💩: i'm gonna disrupt breast milk

Willem didn't mean regular "email" but instead a LootsWeb account, which she had to create and coordinate with his assistant to sign an NDA. A lengthy process that took most of the afternoon, but finally she opened the file he sent her and started reading.

The Oligarch sat at the head of the table, a panoply of small plates in front of him. He grazed slowly at the various pickled items—beets, trout, cabbage, tomato. It seemed to Chloe that Russians only ate food that came from a jar filled with vinegar. Not bad for the diet, she mused, but not as sumptuous as she had come to expect from a man as wealthy as the Oligarch.

"Breast milk," he said, setting his forkful of bitter tomato on the small plate. "You would sell your breast milk?"

"Not mine," Chloe responded, carefully stripping the breading off of the fried chicken breast on her plate. At the first of her periodic lunches with the Oligarch, Chloe hadn't been able to disguise her disgust at Russian cuisine. Since then, the Oligarch had graciously provided her with a KFC combo meal. Chloe had learned that outside of America, everyone thought that Americans exclusively ate KFC and, she considered, they were probably right. The Oligarch had sent an attendant to the Nevsky Prospekt knockoff KFC every week and Chloe wasn't sure if it was a genuine attempt to make her feel more at home or a thinly veiled jab at her heritage. Probably both. "Willem says he's sourced the breast milk, he just needs me as the face."

A wide, inscrutable smile spread across the Oligarch's face. "Tell me, again. What is the problem with American breast milk that needs solving?"

Chloe launched into the pitch and was surprised at the high she felt. Something much sweeter than social media. "Professional women have been at a crossroads with breast milk for as long as I can remember. Formulas are filled with unhealthy additives, and natural breast milk leaves them sitting in an office bathroom painfully pumping their tits into a weird milking machine. It's undignified. That's before even mentioning the constant shortages of formula. Enter UDDR," she said with a flourish of her hand. The Oligarch raised an eyebrow. "I told Willem he should change the name," she added as an aside. "UDDR connects professional women with real, organic human breast milk, delivered quickly and on-demand from an easy-to-use app. Now, professional women don't have to worry about pumping themselves, or the dangerous additives in over-the-counter formulas. They can have natural breast milk delivered as-needed, whether they're at home or on the go."

The Oligarch seemed to consider this as he sliced a chunk of pallid cabbage and brought a forkful to his mouth. He swallowed and said "I'm not certain I understand the business, but your country is a very different culture than my own. That being said, my dear, where do you come in? You are not providing milk, and your children are living thousands of miles away. They are somewhat old for breast milk, yes? Unless," he added with an arched eyebrow, "this is another one of those cultural differences."

Chloe waved off the idea. "No, no, nothing like that. My kids aren't drinking breast milk and, besides, I don't want to cut them in." She leaned in. "Willem has a brilliant idea. He says I have heat, everyone's talking about me since I got banned from socials. Americans are anti-authority by their nature," she quoted the talking points from Willem's pitch packet, "it doesn't matter if that authority is in their best interest, they don't like being told what to do. He thinks there's an interesting loophole. *I'm* not allowed on social media, but there's no rule against me appearing on other feeds. He wants me to be the face. The professional every-mom who this service is perfect for."

"So, what am I here for?"

"Willem needs money," Chloe said. "And your airfield. He wants to talk to you about logistics. Russia has some of the purest breast milk on Earth according to the Worldwide Breastmilk Forum."

The Oligarch leaned back and thought. Chloe reflected how the American culture of wealth was all about efficiency and speed. Seldom was there a pregnant silence, outside of a calculated "power move." The Oligarch seemed to think before he spoke, something that would be viewed as weakness by those with means back home.

"Someone needs to get rich from this new American revolution, no?

Now, Chloe considered for a moment. She hadn't thought this would be so easy. "Exactly."

A wide smile crawled once again across the Oligarch's face. He reached over to shake her hand.

NINE

July 2, 2038 | Washington D.C.

Jay had a room in the West Wing with no windows. He set up lamps, Christmas lights, anything to dull the mind-killing fluorescents. He had a staff of seven reports that sat on Macbooks with headphones. Some of them wrote speeches, tweets, and blog posts. Others edited videos. The two photographers were always in and out of the bunker, following Pablo and snapping shots, only coming back to Photoshop the red from his eyes.

He felt their malaise. Mostly they scrolled through Facebook like the rest of America. Though the company had been bought out by Berkshire-Hathaway for a pittance after the bottom fell out on internet advertising, the website still chugged along: a self-sustaining engine of fury and memes.

Like Jay, his reports thought they were going to the White House to change something. And like them, Jay realized that the system was built to resist change. Ever since Jay's failed PowerPoint, Lupe had started taking away responsibilities from him. First, it was social media.

"We hired a new rockstar named Zoe who is *so* in touch with the youth, so we can take that off your plate," Lupe said cheerfully, motioning towards a person that, to him, looked like a teenager glued to her phone. Then, it was website updates. They were contracting that out. A sub-contractor was taking the email campaign. Lupe always smiled and said the same thing, that she was taking it off his plate. Except, there was nothing much on his plate anymore. He stubbornly held onto speeches but that was only because of an intervention by the First Lady.

At Friday dinner, an old tradition of theirs born in the days when he was in his twenties living on Lily and Pablo's couch in their one-bedroom apartment, which now took place in the family dining room, presided over by an especially mean portrait of Harry Truman, or on nice days, the South Lawn where Pablo's children would play while Jay, Pablo, and Lily drank icy caipirinhas.

Lily was six months pregnant, her hands folded over her belly, wearing linen trousers and a loose lilac blouse. She didn't wear makeup and didn't need to. She was unlike other first ladies, with their designer suits and perfectly coiffed hair. She was *real*. A mom of two with one more on the way. The press was obsessed with her. A young, beautiful woman in the White House after decades of white women reminiscent of the worst kind of middle school vice principal. She noticed he was somewhere else and finally wore him down.

"I don't know why I'm here," he said. "Nobody on staff wants me here. They think because I don't have a college degree from Princeton that I'm a moron. I just feel kind of lost and out of place."

"You're changing the world," she said.

"It doesn't feel that way." He spent his entire week coaching a very bored Billie Eilish through a video explanation of what a monopoly was in the White House's quest to educate people on policy. He spent hours talking her through it, writing and rewriting the script, going through dozens of edits, only for Lupe to can it anyway. He felt like a hamster on a wheel running and running and running.

"I know that Pablo needs you," she said. She took his hand and squeezed it. "I'll talk to him."

The day after, Pablo said in a staff meeting that every talking point had to be routed through Jay or Pablo wouldn't read it.

While it was something, it didn't feel like a win. Everyone knew he had simply cried to Mommy and Daddy. Jay could tell from the looks on their faces. His only qualification was their love.

It was humiliating. His only qualification was Pablo's love. Half of the staffers thought he was Pablo's drug dealer.

The next day, after Lupe had taken videos "off his plate" to concentrate on speeches, he sat in his office with nothing to do. He just looked at videos of rockets blowing up over Loots Town to see if he could glean any information about the closed city. When the phone rang, he picked it up immediately.

"Betteta," he said.

"Hi," an uncertain voice said on the phone. "This is, uh, Felix. I work in the State Department."

"Who?" Jay asked.

"Felix Cohn. I'm Jacky Cohn's great nephew."

"Oh, right." The deal he made. "What can I do for you?"

"I wanted to talk to you about Willem Loots," he said. Jay perked up.

"What about him?"

"I'd rather we meet in person," he said. "It's sensitive information."

Jay entered a low-key bar just off U Street. He looked around. The place was half as full as usual as people fled the brutal D.C. heat for beaches and lake houses. The lobbyists were the loudest, buying rounds of drinks for congressional interns. Reporters always sat at the bar with a book nursing an IPA, pretending at not trying to overhear everybody else. A photograph of Pablo hung on the dart board.

He was not universally beloved.

"Javier," a short, dark-haired man in a neat suit and stylish glasses called out to him from a booth in the corner.

"Felix?" he asked. He nodded. He looked nothing like his great aunt except for the pale blue eyes, incongruous with his olive skin. "Jay," he said, shaking his hand.

"So," Jay said, feeling like this was more of a date than a covert meet-up.

"Beer?" Felix asked.

"A Corona," Jay replied. He wasn't much of a drinker but thought it might take the edge off covert operations. He watched Felix go up to the bar and order. A few drunk lobbyists spoke to him and he was polite, but gave them the brush off. He returned and smiled warmly at Jay.

"What information do you have?" Jay asked, not knowing the operating procedure.

"Willem Loots is working with the Russians," Felix said.

Standard operating procedure: Jumping right in. "That's not the first time I've heard something like that about a political enemy," Jay said, sipping his beer. Felix nodded, like he had been anticipating that answer, and pulled up a document on his phone. The grid listed hundreds of numbers. "What am I looking at?"

"That's Loots's new air fleet," Felix said. Jay thumbed through the document. There were hundreds of entries. "This came from my third cousin at the FAA. Loots built an airfield over there and is registering thousands of planes for international operation."

"If he lives in his own kingdom, why does he need to work with the FAA?"

"Yeah," Felix clicked his tongue. Jay shuddered. Just like Jacky. "Just because he lives in an innovation zone doesn't mean he can fly unregistered airplanes from Loots Town over the United States."

"How do you know it's Russia?"

"They are landing in an airfield outside of St. Petersburg owned by a Russian oligarch."

"What do you think he's doing?"

"Personally," Felix said. "With the authorizations he's requesting? I think he's smuggling weapons."

Jay looked up with alarm. Weapons? Here Jay thought the guy was doing normal rich guy shit like forcing brown kids to build iPhones. "What do you need me for?"

"I can get a team up and running in Pahrump doing recon. Willem Loots won't be able to take a dump without us getting a complete rundown." Felix held out his fist for a fist bump. "You in?"

"How do I know this isn't some elaborate political trap set by your geriatric aunt?" Jay asked.

"You think I didn't run this by her?" Felix said. "That old cow doesn't do anything unless it causes an uptick in her portfolio. A portfolio very heavily invested in Loots tech."

"What's your interest in Loots then?"

"Listen, Loots is dangerous. I know the guy from an internship at McKinsey. He's fucking insane. He's a loose cannon and that makes him the *perfect* Russian asset," Felix said quietly. "I know you have no reason to trust me, but I'm trying to change things too. I'm just trying to do it from the inside. You cowboys need allies too."

Changing things from the outside wasn't working that well.

"Pretty life-and-death stuff for the State Department," Jay said.

Felix smiled again, except with no warmth in his eyes. A company guy for sure.

"You're asking for money," Jay said.

"Give me half a week," Felix said. Jay looked back down at the spreadsheet. Some of the models listed were huge cargo jets, definitely big enough to carry heavy weapons.

Jay took a deep breath. He wasn't sure whose side Felix was on, but hey, the enemy of Willem Loots was a friend of Jay's.

"I do have a discretionary account I can tap," Jay said, and they shook hands.

TEN

July 2 - 3, 2038 | Loots Town

After the guards scanned their identification, they motioned for Sasha to park her car in an old gas station retrofitted as a barracks and climb into the back of a black Humvee. The guard pulled onto what was once Highway 160 through the looming perimeter fence. Men with assault rifles patrolled the top, smoking cigarettes and spitting onto the desert twenty feet below.

The fence formed a quarter-mile perimeter around Loots Town. Sasha noticed sage brush, Joshua trees, and yucca growing through picked-over homes, ratty trailers, and bombed out 7-Elevens that peppered the no man's land between the fence and the spear of Loots Tower rising up from between two enormous conjoining white domes.

"Two balls and a dick," Matt muttered. "Subtle." The driver shot him a look and slid into an opening built into the base of one of the domes. Guards opened the door and ushered Matt and Sasha into separate sides of what looked like a garage. Uniformed workers hauled crates and goods from trucks to drones. The guard pushed her into an empty all white room. The guards were easy to spot—armed and dressed in black fatigues with the word Loots emblazoned on the front.

"Hand," a guard asked with her arm outstretched, and then grabbed Sasha's index finger and pricked it with an oblong white device.

"What was that for?"

"It's just part of onboarding," the guard said. She then handed over a Loots Tablet with an information form and a detailed NDA. Sasha scanned it. Kim would have been impressed.

"You sign or you leave," the guard said coldly.

Sasha signed and the guard directed her through another door.

Sasha was relieved to see Matt on the other side. A screen read "Welcome to Loots Town: The Future of Wonder." The spherical walls were made of high-definition screens showing landscapes of birds flying through the air, the ocean smashing against the rocks blanketed with squirming crabs, a Loots spacecraft orbiting the moon, images of nebulas and red dwarfs from Loots's Galileo deep space telescope, happy families hand in hand in an idyllic, manicured park. Beautiful women stood everywhere, welcoming other disoriented visitors coming from other white rooms.

"I could have thought of something better," Sasha grumbled to Matt.

"Dmitry said I'd like you," Sasha heard a polished British accent from behind her. A tall, thin woman with long dark hair and a stylish wrap dress smiled at her.

Sasha watched the woman. She was beautiful but there was something strange about her. Her brilliant purple iris of her right eye spun in different directions, almost like a lens zooming in and out on Sasha. She lacked the regular human twitches and movements, the hum of biology at work.

"You know my brother?"

"Mariko," she said. Holding her hand out. Sasha took it.

"I'm the senior vice President of Loots Town operations. It's so nice to meet you" She ignored Matt.

Two other beautiful women joined Mariko, forming a triangle around Sasha and Matt. "Come," she said and turned to exit the room through a seamless door that appeared on one side of the sphere. As they walked through, Sasha looked for seams. "The whole room can be a door," she explained. "Spaces shouldn't be littered with corners, entrances, and exits, it should be malleable and transformative."

Sasha couldn't help gasping when a set of automatic doors opened and Loots Town spread before them. Twisting Gaudi-like glass and steel buildings stacked on top of each other with balconies looking over lush green spaces and swimming pools. Loots Tower perfectly bisected the space. The city smelled of jasmine. While it was 112 degrees in the desert outside, inside it was a perfect 75.

"UV and temperature controlled," Mariko said, pointing at the top of the domes, almost see-through except for slender white veins. "You can get a tan without the heatstroke. We change it throughout the town depending on what activity you're engaging in." Sometimes text rippled across the perfectly blue sky, quotes from Willem Loots, memes, rainbows, the number 69.

Mariko led Matt and Sasha down a series of stairwells to the main arteries of Loots Town. There were no street signs or traffic. Everybody seemed to know where they were going. Pools dotted the landscape along with exotic and colorful flowers (imported from Willem's home country, Mariko said). Fat prehistoric palm trees the likes of which Sasha had not seen in Vegas or Los Angeles reached towards the top of the dome.

Without Sasha realizing it, Mariko had stopped them in front of Loots Tower. The tour was over. Smooth black glass curved around the doorway and into the sky like a finger pointed towards the sun.

"This is only the beginning," Mariko finished with a flourish. Sasha had barely listened to what she'd said. Mariko rarely blinked.

"Wow, cool," Sasha said, unsure how to respond. "So, where is my brother?" she asked Mariko.

"Ah, unfortunately he's done for the day. He lives over in Yurts Town." At Sasha's confused expression, she continued, "It's part of our Phase 2 plans" with a shrug as if that explained it all.

"Can I go there then?" Sasha asked.

"Oh no, I wish you could, but there is an outer-dome curfew after the unfortunate military attack."

"It's six PM," Sasha said. "Are you saying I can't leave?"

Mariko winked. "Don't worry. We have accommodations available for you and your friend tonight."

"Okay," Sasha said, feeling light-headed.

"Oh," Mariko clapped her hands together, looking up. "It's beginning."

Sasha followed her gaze. She didn't know if the domes enhanced the sunset, or if it was particularly beautiful that night, but the reds, oranges, and pinks filled the dome with a warm light. A hundred or so people sat by the lapping waves of the gentle bay cocooned around the base of the Loots Tower. More and more people joined them as a few electronic chords played—the Loots national anthem, written by Daft Punk, and a video of a rocket appeared, embedded into the sunset. Audio piped in from mission control and the spectators counted down until the rocket launched itself into the air, accompanied by an exciting jolt deep in the earth. The crowd cheered as the thin rocket seen on both the video feed and in the physical distance against the Spring Mountains soared into the sky.

The accommodations, it turned out, were on the 80th floor of Loots Tower. She was so high she could see the city of Las Vegas carpeting the desert floor over the mountains. The suite had three bedrooms, a pool table, a wrap-around television, a full bar, Jacuzzis, even a plunge pool. Everything was tastefully decorated in modern black and white.

Sasha poured herself a healthy portion of whiskey and sat on the couch. She was afraid to touch anything, as though her grubby fingers would break all these beautiful things. She recognized a painting on the wall as a Vermeer.

Matt and Sasha sat next to each other side by side on the couch. He took her whiskey out of her hand.

"I thought you were sober," she said faintly.

"Not here," he said, draining the glass and then looking at the crystal reflecting the light. "This is too nice for me to hold," he said.

"I know."

"I feel very conflicted right now," he said.

"Join the club." Rich people were supposed to be evil. Murderers. Loots Town, however, was perfect. While the rest of the world was falling apart, this place seemed full of... possibility. And yet something didn't strike Sasha as right about it. It was weird. They sat side by side for a while. She could feel the warmth of his hand next to hers, barely touching, on the couch.

"Do you want to make out?" Sasha asked.

"Wait, really?" he said, and she kissed him. She craved something normal and familiar, something she knew how to do with her hands and body. "You know I've always had a crush on you," he breathed.

"Shut up," Sasha said. She removed his glasses, then his shirt, and ran her hands over his bony rib cage.

The next morning Sasha slipped out of the soft bed and dressed in a simple white outfit she found stocked in a dresser. She left Matt fast asleep in the sunrise.

Downstairs Mariko was waiting for her.

"Good night?" Mariko said with a glint in her eye, like she knew.

"I'm ready to see Dima," Sasha said.

"Certainly," she said. She called over a small blonde girl who didn't look at Sasha and told her to ready a Pegasus for a trip out to Yurts Town. She motioned Sasha over and put her arm through Sasha's. "Before we do, I'd like to run something by you." She guided Sasha over to plush couches. They sat.

"You're the one who turned in Kim Kardashian," Mariko said with no vocal inflection or facial expression.

"Read my Wikipedia," Sasha said. "I'm an activist."

Mariko smiled with no warmth and activated a console on the table between them, pulling up documents on a holographic projection. "Activism, huh? It looks like you're a pizza delivery gig worker on a $3.25 per delivery pay scale. Tell me, does that even cover gas?"

"How do you know that?" Sasha asked.

"I bought the data from the company," Mariko said. "It seems like you languish, doing drugs, getting too drunk with your friends, and that Kim Kardashian put you on the blacklist before the President murdered her." Sasha noted the word murdered.

"So, there is a blacklist?" Sasha had heard about an encrypted app the elite used to cancel people amongst themselves, spread word about workers they couldn't trust, collaborate on talking points about world affairs, and insider trade, but of course, who would tell her about the app's existence? Willem Loots, she guessed.

"You have no future. Our algorithms say that you will probably die around 40. Cancer. The drugs you do are impure, and your white blood cell count is up." At Sasha's expression, Mariko added: "Your blood, remember? The only light in your life seems to be your niece, Maya," Mariko said, pulling up Maya's school picture. "A good student, but she is sick as well. Everybody in today's America is sick."

"What do you want?" Sasha said.

Mariko drummed her long fingernails on her Loots Tablet and then swiped the holographic records. "I knew you were smart. Dima is clever, but you're smart. Cultured," she said. "You can read between the lines. Shame you have no future in the new world order. Unless..." Mariko trailed off. Sasha raised her eyebrows.

"I can offer you a position right now as the Press Secretary of Loots Town. It would pay 2.76 LootCoin a month which is the equivalent of $500,000 per year. You would be provided with apartments here, of course, that I believe will be to your satisfaction."

"Why me?" Sasha asked. "I'm damaged goods."

"That's precisely why," Mariko said.

Sasha said nothing, and then: "Can I use the bathroom?"

"Certainly," Mariko said without skipping a beat. "Right through there." A stairwell led underground into a depot where driverless electric cars parked waiting for passengers. A man spoke on a cell phone quickly, ducking into a car. It pulled into a tunnel. A neon sign pointed towards restrooms. Once inside, she locked the door and fished her cell phone out of her pocket. She had zero bars. She connected to Loots WiFi and found that none of her regular apps would load. When she opened her text messaging app, the phone automatically directed her to the Loots messenger app.

A panic took hold. The city was a closed loop. Sasha was trapped, at the whim of the woman above, who knew everything about her and wanted something from her.

ELEVEN

July 10, 2038 | Санкт-Петербург, Россия

"This audience growth rate is not good enough, Layla," Chloe said to a cartoon representation of Layla, the senior social media specialist for UDDR. "I want a copy of a new strategy by Monday with targets, KPIs, and a paid search budget request." Chloe delighted in ordering people around. Even in the cartoon metaverse, where Willem insisted all meetings take place, it was satisfying to watch her avatar, who was taller and had bigger tits than Layla's, shake her fist while a little exclamation point appeared on top of Layla's short, stupid head.

"I mean," Chloe recited her talking points. "There are new mothers every single day, and as a previous one myself, they want their bodies back, their lives back, while also caring for their child. In fact, do some question posts on that, get people's experiences, repost their stories. I see a whole new branding: 'Care for You.'" People love to be told to "self-care," to excuse reckless materialism or narcissism as being actually healthy.

God, she had missed posting. She still technically couldn't post, but she directed people to post. She redlined all the UDDR social media copy until it was perfect. People said social media gave you mental illness, that it gave you "fear of missing out," that it divided people into multiple personalities. Chloe didn't understand why that was a bad thing. She liked to be divided because that meant that if someone got one piece of her, there was always another one wriggling out of the darkness. The people who write those studies about social media have never been poor, she thought, so they don't know how sweet it is to be rich. They just expect things.

Willem was the one who pushed her to set tough goals for UDDR. He said the success of the company was integral to their plan. At first, she thought it would be a pain. The truth was, she had never been happier. She might be exiled and single, but for once, she called the shots. UDDR was *hers*. She was, dare she say it, a girlboss. It felt good, for the first time in her life, to not be wholly enslaved to men and their penises. She was working on a monthly report to her investors, who, yes, were men, but they wanted to know about her business acumen, not her waist size. Willem expected spreadsheets full of data and glossy materials! She was in command of her own destiny. She felt giddy, like a TED Talk. If she had known that being a girlboss would contribute to the destruction of the Communist President, she would have started way back when he was treated as a joke candidate on CNNBC.

Chloe threw a tasteful blazer over her burgundy blouse and trousers before heading out into the St. Petersburg sunshine. It seemed like none of the Russians were working, they were just shopping, lounging in parks reading books, and drinking vodka with their friends on the banks of the Neva. This place wasn't so bad with its colorful palaces, manicured gardens, and bustling shopping districts. It was like Paris, except cheaper. A handsome Russian in his twenties winked at her as she passed by. She felt his eyes on her ass. What a blessedly normal feeling, being checked out by a hot guy on a summer day.

Chloe entered the subway. She loved that the subways here looked like grand ballrooms. She would never ride the disgusting public transportation in America where, inevitably, she would see a homeless man jerking off, but here everybody was quiet, reading books, and leaning against polished marble columns. A dignified means of transport.

She got off at Vasileostrovskaya and began walking towards the shipyard. The wet nurses, Chloe had branded them Milk Partners, worked in a warehouse on the port that shuttled milk back to Kaliningrad on its way to the USA. Why Russian milk? Chloe wrote in a glossy business plan. Frankly, it's cleaner. All milk partners are on an organic Mediterranean diet, a regimen of vitamins, and spend one hour on a Peloton in the morning and one hour in a yoga class at night. Did they actually do that? Chloe wasn't sure. She did post thin, but still healthy, stock pictures of women all over the communication materials. Perfect mothers, with pillowy, soft breasts.

Chloe wanted to drop in and make sure they were maintaining the rigorous regimen she was marketing to weepy soccer moms in Westchester.

Her heels clicked along the sidewalks leading her through the squat industrial buildings with smokestacks rising from their innards until she reached the shore. Barges sat in port loaded with shipping containers. The UDDR office, or the P.O. box associated with the company, was located on Kozhevennaya Liniya. The street was less trafficked than the others in the area and she could see why. What was supposed to be the worldwide headquarters of her company was a mossy, neoclassical structure weathered with age. She pulled at a door and had to use all her strength to wedge an opening for her to slip through. Crates and equipment were stacked neatly in the damp, dark hallways leaving a passageway barely big enough for her to squeeze through. A single lightbulb suspended from the ceiling hung near Cyrillic lettering. She heard women speaking. Chloe straightened her blazer and walked towards it with purpose.

"Hello, partners!" she said, holding out a few gift bags she put together the night before with whatever healthy snack options she could scrounge from the local grocery store. Her smile faded when she saw a few women with lined faces, smoking cigarettes and playing chess at a card table set up in what looked like a break room. Where was the yoga? Where were the Pelotons?

One of them stood and started yelling in Russian. When

Chloe shook her head and said in loud, slow English "I don't know Russian," another woman stood up and shoved her.

"No need for that!" Chloe said, stumbling back but holding her ground.

"Out! Out!" they yelled.

"Fine! I'm keeping the snacks then," she said before turning on her heels and leaving. Before the exit, she paused at a crate marked UDDR. It didn't look like the refrigerated technology she touted that kept breast milk fresh on its journey to America. She heard another scream from one of the Russian women, turned and gave them the finger before marching back outside.

Chloe perhaps didn't like everything about being a girlboss.

Twelve

July 11, 2038 | Loots Town International Airfield

Through her ocular implant, Mariko could see the cargo plane land. The scan revealed the weight of the plane, the names and files of both pilots, the number of humans onboard, and text of the flight manifest. Audio piped in between the pilot and Loots International air traffic control.

The feed wavered for a moment and she knew that he could see and hear it all too. The content of her brain was not her own. What was a person if they were more than biology, but less than technology? She thought about that a lot. She didn't know if it was a bug in her technology or her human brain churning.

As the plane landed and taxied towards the opening that led underground, to the tunnels, she barked orders at the waiting workers who sprang into action, hopping into forklifts and navigating them through the deafening sound of the jet engines towards the yawning opening at the back of the plane. A worker loaded a crate onto the back of a cart. She approached it and wiped her hand across the smooth wood of the crate stamped with Cyrillic lettering.

Open it, green text displayed across her field of vision. She positioned her hands on either edge of the crate and grunted as she popped it open. She removed refrigerated containers marked as breast milk to reveal dozens of oiled AK-400s.

Mariko heard laughing.

A large man appeared from the innards of the plane. He wore fatigues packed with knives, handguns, grenades, and radio equipment. An unwieldy beard reached the top of his chest. A scar zigzagged across his nose to a cloudy brown eye. He looked her up and down and his mouth twisted into a smile. A wolf and a half-moon icon was ironed onto his chest. Chechnya.

Men ducked out of the plane behind him. The Chechen looked around the runway as workers began to unload the airplane. He let out a low whistle.

"So, this is America, eh?" Then a moment later, spat on the ground. "Looks like a shithole to me." He laughed, and the rest of his men followed suit.

Thirteen

July 13, 2038 | Ft. Cathouse

Jay noticed the palm trees, skinny, anemic, and half-dead, that lined the drab streets in the shadow of the Strip. The glowing, larger-than-life thoroughfare of hotels was incredible in its beauty and magnitude but, what he noticed more, was how that light was drawn from the very city that surrounded it. A city beaten by reality, while also full of life. But not the good kind—desperate, clawing life.

Jay had built the public framework for defunding the police, but it looked different on the ground of a poor American city. The annual budget awarded cities with money to advertise drug treatment programs, free college, jobs for ex-cons, and other civil programs to help people, but he saw none of that, despite a line item that specifically awarded Vegas with hundreds of millions of dollars for these programs and their advertising. Instead, he saw advertisements for armed neighborhood patrols and personal injury firms offering to sue armed neighborhood patrols and cocaine dispensary nightclubs with special guest Tiesto.

Then of course, a billboard reading "Come to Loots Town, the city of wonder," with Willem Loots himself handing a wicker basket of food to starving children on a grungy street corner. "Free buses straight from Circus Circus" it read underneath the image.

"Can you drive faster?" Jay said to the driver, who maneuvered south on the 15 towards Pahrump.

A few days earlier, Jay sat at his laptop, flanked by his team of assistants, busy with *his* work that Lupe had delegated to them. He played Solitaire on his phone. If he won another game in a row, he would get a deck with a beach painted on it. The new goals that made up his professional life.

Lupe poked her head in the door. "Jay, a word?" Jay closed his phone and looked up at her, bleary eyed. His boredom had made him tired.

"What's up?" he asked, expecting her to somehow delegate his Solitaire game to somebody else. With a glance, the assistants scurried out and Lupe sat without invitation. This self-styled champion of the poor wore a Dior pantsuit that was quadruple the price of most Americans' rent.

"I was looking over the line items for your discretionary fund, and I noticed this outlay for a team in Nevada?"

"It's for a street team we're building for voter outreach," Jay lied. "Nevada is a swing state."

"Hm," she said. "Who's running there?"

She was trying to catch him in a lie. "It is my discretionary fund for my personal projects, so," he gave her a dazzling smile. "Maybe check Politico."

"I will," she said coldly. "If this has anything to do with Willem Loots..." she began.

"I'm actually going to a training in a few days to pump up the volunteers," he said. "I'll send you pics."

"So great to see you taking an interest in the midterms," she said, "So excited to hear more about this important grassroots work."

The minute she left he booked a ticket to Vegas and a few days later found himself in an old Kmart in North Las Vegas, squirming in his seat, waiting for the moment to take a selfie with the field organizers and post it to his Instagram. Lupe immediately liked it.

Then he called Felix.

Felix's base of operations in Ft. Cathouse, a few miles of territory nestled between anti-vaxxers and batches of outsiders that bloomed in this new lawless territory—polygamists, Scientologists, Branch Davidians, people that didn't fit.

The main square, done up like a Western trading post. Women called out to the population of mostly men from second story windows and blew them kisses. A guy dressed like a cowboy promised an "Oregon Trail" two-day experience where cowboys went up against robotic bandits and Indian tribes on horseback. People openly did cocaine on the sidewalk off small silver spoons bought from trading posts. A holographic Bon Jovi played on a stage attended by a drunk, screaming, dancing crowd. Jay entered a saloon and was directed up a narrow staircase into a red carpeted hallway where straights humped against wood-paneled walls. He stopped at number 23.

"Jay," Felix answered the door, his sleeves rolled up, fiddling a Juul between his fingers. "Good to see you," he said and motioned Jay inside.

The bed, dresser, television, and desk were all pushed into different corners.

"Nothing should be where it seems," Felix said with a shrug when he noticed Jay looking. A computer set-up with several monitors with video feeds and cascading lines of code was set on a plastic table. A boy who looked no older than seventeen sucked on a grapefruit vape and typed away. Various pieces of equipment were draped on every surface. Listening devices, cameras, hard drives, advanced GPS systems, sat phones, keys to various off-road vehicles, and then junk food, chips, packages of cigarettes. Whiskey. Adderall.

Taxpayer dollars at work.

"So," Jay said, clapping his hands together. "What do you have for me?"

"Do you want a drink?" Felix asked in response.

"No," Jay said. Felix turned and poured himself one. "Felix. What's going on?"

Felix turned and threw the cap of the whiskey bottle at the

teenager. He tore his headphones off. "Give Jay a status report, will you?" he asked. The pimply teenager wiped sweat from his face and put a hand through his spongey black hair. Jay stared at him.

"Who the fuck is this kid?" he asked Felix. He wondered how much they were paying him.

"This *kid* graduated from MIT at 16," the kid said with a high-pitched nasally voice, "And maybe your only chance at getting a look inside Loots Town."

"Wait," Jay said. "You haven't even gotten inside yet?"

"Loots invites hackers to try and break into his computer systems, that's how confident he is," Felix said. "It'll take time."

"What have you been doing the past few weeks?" Jay said. "I've given you a hundred thousand dollars!"

Felix produced a manila envelope stamped with red text reading "EYES ONLY" and fastened at the top with tamper-proof tape. Jay tore it open. He rifled through the contents, finding a number of satellite photos of Loots Town. Jay pulled them close to his face, scrutinizing them.

"I could have gotten these on Google Maps," Jay said.

"Loots Town is a locked box, no information gets in or gets out. It's one thing to gather intel somewhere where there are people just working for a paycheck. These Willem cultists are the real deal. They're devoted. We need someone inside and no one is talking. If I push too hard, they'll know we're sniffing and then we're fucked."

"This is intel you'd get from Reddit detectives living in their mom's basements," Jay said. "QAnon retirees could have done a better job."

"Take a closer look," Felix said.

Jay examined the satellite imagery at different zoom levels and an attached report. He skimmed it.

"Where did you get this?" Jay asked.

"Kenny couldn't get into Loots's system, but he *did* get into air traffic control at Loots International and skimmed some documents off the top," Felix said.

"The kid's name is Kenny?" Jay asked.

“I’m 19!” he whined.

“I was his counselor at Jewish Day Camp,” Felix shrugged. “He’s safe.”

It was suspected to be part of Loots’s privatized space program, but Jay took a look at a manifest for an international cargo flight from Kaliningrad. Jay looked up from the document, his face awash in confusion.

"Breast milk?"

Jay did have a drink then, downstairs at a bar called the Chicken Ranch. He watched a dozen men and women line up for a few drunk college guys up from Vegas. Some of the lineup were robotic, Jay could tell from the glitchy movement of their hands as they ran their fingers over their belly and lacy lingerie. The boys seemed most interested in the AI, “glitch queens” they were called. Jay had read about this. Men flocked to the innovation zones to live out their most shameful thoughts with a soft conscious-less body who couldn’t file assault charges or write about the experience in an online essay. One of the boys went with a glitch queen, the other with a redhead named Rosie.

Jay wondered if this was because Pablo was elected or if it would have happened anyway. America was a movie set built for consumers to live out their dreams with no laws, no ambitions, because people knew there was no future, only women that UCLA frat guys chose to fuck or kill, depending on their machinery. Jay shook his head and looked at a printout.

UDDR was a spinoff of Loots Technologies and headquartered inside Loots Town so, conveniently, he didn’t have to register the company with any state. The only proof the company existed was social media accounts and a “powered by SquareSpace” website mostly devoted to the biography of its CEO, Chloe Thibodeaux, Hunter Meadows’s ex-wife and former Democratic-Republican influencer darling. He remembered a clip of her from the election from Fox News saying that Pablo Lopez made her skin break out. In Russian exile, she recently got dropped from all her remaining endorsement deals for mocking Kim Kardashian's execution. Jay considered that maybe Lupe's big push for social media legislation hadn't been completely useless. Not that Thibodeaux had any remaining relevance in the States anyway. She was a punchline these days. A punchline sending planes of breast milk to Loots Town from Russia.

"I'm telling you," Felix said, swaying in his seat across from Jay, very drunk. "The Russian angle is really starting to make sense."

Jay rolled his eyes. "For the first time in a hundred years we have a fucking peace deal with Russia." The two countries were going to denuclearize. It was a huge foreign policy win that the APP was running on in the midterms. The End of the Forever War.

"That's what they want you to think," Felix said, leaning in. Jay leaned back. He was wasted, the skin under his eyes puffy, and he smelled like old milk. Is this where Jay's discretionary fund was going? One piece of questionable intel, a teenager, and Felix's bar tab?

Jay's phone rang. He dug it out of his pocket. A picture of Lupe picking her nose flashed. "One minute," he told Felix and answered. "Hey, what's up?"

"Hey, world traveler!" Lupe said cheerfully. "I hope you took Airborne! How is Nevada?"

"So great," he said. "Everyone is working hard." A woman in a yellow jumpsuit with holes cut to reveal her bare breasts made mewing sounds into a radio rig. Jay tried to cover the microphone as best he could.

"What was that?" Lupe asked.

"Nothing," Jay said. "It's a little loud outside the campaign office."

"I wanted to ask you something," Lupe said. "I looked it up and it's funny. We already have outreach operations in Nevada. I'm just curious why you didn't contribute to those."

"I'm not ready to share what I'm working on, but as soon as I am I'll be happy to brief you," Jay said, getting irritated.

"I am looking forward to it, there's just one more thing. I'm sure you can clear it up," she sounded positively gleeful. "You have an outlay to Company Renovations, LLC. Do you know that's a CIA shell company?"

Jay looked over at Felix, hunched over the bar, leering at an oiled–up shirtless dude serving shots in test tubes. Guess he subcontracted the espionage to the spooks. Sloppy. Jay felt the rage build. What a fucking idiot.

"I will certainly look into that," he said, calmly.

"I have no doubt you will," she said. "I already told Pablo and he has revoked your discretionary fund and your security clearance. We will need you back in the West Wing ASAP. The President wants to keep you on a strict, how do you say it, breakfast sandwich basis."

Jay froze. His brain not quite working. He was done. Lupe finally won. A cowboy walked by and looked Jay up and down.

"Hey man," he said. He pulled out a switchblade and dug it into a bag of white powder and held it up for Jay. "Want any?"

"Jay?" Lupe said. "What the hell was that? Where are you?" Jay hung up.

"Why the fuck not?" he said. He hung up and snorted his first noseful of cocaine.

Fourteen

July 14, 2038 | Loots Town

Every day was the same. Sasha got up, went downstairs, asked the concierge if she could see Dima that day, the concierge promised Sasha she would check and get back as soon as possible. Sasha went back upstairs, and never heard back.

When Sasha came back from Mariko's job offer (or threat), Mariko informed her Dima couldn't see her, but maybe he could tomorrow. She allowed Sasha to make a phone call to Olga.

"You're where?" Olga asked.

"Loots Town," Sasha said. "Put Maya on the phone." She heard rustling and Olga's coughs.

"Hello?" Maya asked.

"Hey," Sasha relaxed. "Finding your dad is going to take a little more time, okay?"

"How much more?"

"I'm not really sure," Sasha said. Maya paused for a long time.

"Please come back, okay?"

"I will," Sasha said. "With his signature. No more shots," Sasha promised.

"No more shots," Maya said.

Then a week passed. Then ten days. She hadn't seen Mariko

since that morning. She only spoke with hotel staff. They didn't let her out of the tower. She was imprisoned in a two-story suite with a plunge pool.

"This isn't so bad," Matt said, naked on the deck in sunglasses. "Though I hope my cat is okay," he said, a little nervous.

Sex. Drinking. Food. Sleep. Plunge pool. Repeat. The days started to merge into the next.

"I've probably lost my job," she said, swigging tequila straight from the bottle that was always magically refilled while they were sleeping.

"I bet my Twitter is blowing up," Matt said. He leaned over and kissed her neck. She leaned into it, closing her eyes.

Sex. Drinking. Food. Sleep. Plunge pool. Repeat.

She didn't even bother going downstairs that morning. She picked up a Loots Tablet and rang downstairs from the plunge pool.

"Is it Dima's day off yet?" she said, still a little drunk.

"Actually, yes, miss," the concierge said brightly. "If you can be downstairs in ten minutes, your brother is on his way!"

Sasha nearly dropped the tablet in the water. She got dressed in the pair of clothes she had worn into Loots Town and Matt did the same. She splashed water on her face, hoping the coolness would leach the hangover out of her face. She cursed. If they told her about this earlier, she would have ordered an IV.

When the elevator doors clicked open, Dima stood waiting for her, chatting with Mariko.

He had gained weight, in a good way. His shoulders and arms were lean and muscled. He wore different clothing than the others, crisp jeans and a button-up blue shirt made of a strong and durable material. His long blonde hair had grown out and was pulled into a ponytail. He had a full beard and tanned face. Sasha smiled despite herself. After so many days of worrying, she could relax. He looked healthy.

Sasha ran up and hugged him, feeling like a child. He squeezed her and then had a good look at her.

"You look like shit," he laughed. His blue eyes sparkled in amusement.

"I'm hungover," she said.

"Welcome to Loots Town," he replied.

"You know I've been waiting for nearly two weeks," she said.

"What can I say?" he said, "Been busy. Has it been really rough here in the Loots Tower penthouses?" She punched his shoulder playfully as he recoiled, laughing. Then his eyes darkened when he saw Matt behind her. He stiffened his shoulders.

"Hey Dima," Matt said shyly. "You look good, man."

Dima eyed Matt dispassionately before declaring: "So, this is still your game, huh?"

"Dude, I'm checking in on you!"

"Dude, then why don't I believe you?" Dima mocked. Sasha eyed the two of them. Dima looked defiant, angry, while Matt stared down at the ground. Mariko watched the two, her strange eye zooming in and out on each of them individually.

"Dmitry, why not take your sister to the flats? I'll know she'll want to see what you're working on." Mariko said.

"Sounds good," Matt said, grabbing Sasha's hand and squeezing. Dima watched him touch her.

"Oh, I'm sorry," Mariko said, "Yurts Town is for residents and their family members only. Are you a family member?" She smiled but her eyes were ice cold.

Matt pulled Sasha aside and held her hand as he spoke in a low voice: "I don't think you should go off with him alone."

"I'll be fine," Sasha said, squeezing his hand then letting it go. Sasha felt Dima's eyes on them.

"Yeah, I am her brother after all, how much safer can she be?" A look passed between Matt and Dima before Mariko instructed two men with slung assault rifles to escort Matt to the pachinko room.

Dima displayed the Loots Town glow, the utopian freshness that originated in the eyes and reverberated through the body in otherworldly waves. He led Sasha into the depths of Loots Tower, where a maze of unmarked hallways with the same seamless metal alloy as the visitor's center glowed. Finally, it opened into a recognizable parking garage and Dima motioned Sasha to get into a blue Pegasus. Sasha buckled into the passenger seat and Dima drove through a series of underground tunnels.

After a time, the tunnel opened up into the open desert and Dima sped across the valley. Sasha looked behind her at the dick and balls of Loots Town baking in the sun. The last few weeks in the temperature-controlled dome, she had forgotten they lived in the desert and that it was hot.

He parked the Pegasus next to a sandstone rock formation that jutted out of the desert like an undulating wave right below the peaks of the Spring Mountains. Sections of the rock were blown out and replaced with weathered white doors that barely fit man-made caves that had once housed miners. Hundreds of rusted over cans had created little lakes of fossilized trash. Chunks of mining equipment lay discarded in the heat. As though the miners had simply woken up from a nap and deserted the camp forever, which is probably what they did.

Dima wordlessly made his way to a makeshift workbench lined with dusty mason jars and uncapped one of them. He smelled it then held it up to the sun. He moved onto the next one. The workbench formed an island in a web of adobe bricks hardening in the sun. At the far end of the rock, about fifty yards from the workbench, a half-built structure formed a rectangle around a cave opening. Sasha walked over and saw a piece of graph paper nailed to an old wooden post. Dima was building a nave—vaulted ceilings, reclaimed stained glass decorated with crosses and shards of a bloodied Jesus leaned against one of the four-foot adobe walls.

"Are you building a church?" Sasha called out to Dima. He looked into another mason jar and tossed it into a waste bin.

"No, you fucking moron. I'm building a house."

"Do you know how to build a house?"

"I know how to use YouTube." Dima walked back over as he examined another jar. Sand had sunk to the bottom with clay pooled on top. He dipped his fingers in the jar, swirled the mud around, and nodded. An explosion sounded somewhere across the valley. Sasha turned to see a plume of smoke rising toward Ash Meadows. Dima walked to stand next to Sasha.

"Jabba the Hutt experience," he said, shrugging.

"So, this is yours?" Sasha asked. He pulled out a slip of paper and unfolded it. A deed with his name on it. "It really is," she marveled at the shithole, halfway to becoming a home.

"Loots needed carpenters bad," Dima said. "We struck a deal."

"So, this is where the workers will live?" she asked.

"This," Dima said. "Is where the Women as Warrior retreats and spiritual experiences will be housed. Earth houses for all!" He pointed in the direction in the far valley where the vineyard used to be. A village of geodesic domes grew out of the ground like warts. "We still need HVAC guys though. Let me know if you have any recommendations."

"You really are doing well here," she said.

"Vegas is... full of demons," he said. "The whole point of Loots Town is to exorcize those demons. I just needed out, and some structure."

Sasha smiled. "I'm proud of you."

"Now, what brings you here?" Dima said. "Please don't say Matt brought you on some podcast bullshit."

"Why do you hate him so much?" Sasha asked.

"I hate podcasts," he said, leaning against the workbench.

"It's better than delivering pizzas," she said.

"What's so wrong with delivering pizza?"

She shook her head. "Maya. That's the reason I'm here."

Dima stopped and looked at her, very still. "What about her?"

"Maya needs surgery." Dima shielded his eyes and examined the paper. "It'll practically cure the diabetes. Manage it so she doesn't have to rely on Insulin. All you need to do is sign some papers. I'll come up with the money somehow."

Dima shook his head. "If Maya needs surgery, bring her here."

"Dima," Sasha exclaimed, "No. It's okay for you, and I'm so happy for you, but this place is... *scary* for, like, a kid." She hadn't thought about it before, and she had to admit Loots Town was beautiful and luxurious, but there was something strange and ominous about it. She didn't want Maya here.

"There's a hospital right over there with state of the art, and free, medical treatment for residents." Dima pointed at a squat building in the distance,

"No fucking way," she said. "That's the Gold Town Casino, not a hospital."

"The hospitals in Vegas are shit."

"Then I'll go to LA!"

"On Medicare For Kids? Please. She's my child. I was going to come get her soon anyway. I'm better now. Thank you for looking out for her but this is the place for us."

"Where is she going to school?" Sasha asked.

"I'll teach her," he said. "What else does she even need to know?"

"Jesus," Sasha looked up to the sky. "Where is your fucking generator, Dima? Where is the heat in the winter? Where is the shower? The closest water?" The cave was beautiful, it was true, and he seemed interested in building a floor, but the desert was unfriendly. "Matt was right. I shouldn't have come out here. I knew you'd just make everything worse."

"Matt, huh," Dima said. "He told you he always had a crush on you, didn't he?" Sasha said nothing. Dima laughed, rubbed his temple, then said: "You want to know why I hate him? Listen to Episode #107." He held out his iPhone and a pair of earbuds.

Recorded selection from Deep Gate episode 107: SAD SAD OPIOID CITY

MATT: I'm Matt Fisher.

LISETTE: And I'm Lisette Gorski.

MATT & LISETTE: And this is Deep Gate!

MATT: Now, lovely listeners, this episode is especially important to me, because it's not just about the Opioid epidemic, about the forgotten cohort, it's about my own life. So, before we get into the Sacklers, and fucking fentanyl, I want to talk about me. I grew up in Las Vegas, fucking shit poor, and COVID-28 closed schools for two shiteating years in my school. School was my only respite from home. My dad split town to have a new family in Dallas. Mom was a checked-out gambler, who left me with my aunt more than she was home. My girlfriend Denise got me into heroin. I found out she was fucking her dealer, and I wanted to stay with her, to understand her, so I started using too, and it was just... so much better than reality, it was just me and her. Us versus the world, floating through the world. We didn't know she was pregnant until she was basically giving birth to a preemie girl doing cartwheels in her emaciated belly. An Uber dropped us off at the hospital and she gave birth to our baby girl via emergency c-section. I held her hand through it, and you know what we did afterwards? We shot up in the bathroom and left the hospital. Our little baby died two days later, alone, frightened, all because of this stuff. I will never forgive myself for that. I've done many things, many fucked up shitty things, but that haunts me. I don't even remember her face. My baby girl. Maya.

Sasha ripped out the earbuds and threw them into the desert. "You see?" Dima said. "You see why I wanted to fucking escape?"

Matt sat in the pachinko chair staring at his phone as Loots Town residents pulled down on the pulleys and watched the screen flash and flicker. A luminous utopian city, and it was still just like Vegas at the end of the day. He stood at the sight of Sasha.

"No reception but it's just a habit," he said, gesturing at his phone. She didn't say anything and started heading towards the entrance. "Whoa, whoa, Sasha, what did you see?" He said, racing forward and positioning his body in front of her. He tried to take her hand and she wrenched it back.

"We can go now," Sasha said. "Dima finally released us."

Sasha didn't speak for the entire journey to the car, and from there to the Chicken Shack. Sasha ordered three shots, a White Claw, and a line of cocaine.

"I'm going to get a room" Sasha said, doing the line set out by a busty barmaid. "You can get a cab back to Vegas."

"What happened?" Matt said. "Whatever it was, we can get through it together." He couldn't stop prying, trying to tug at her life for more *material*.

"Okay," she said, buzzing on the coke. "Tell me about Episode 107."

"Oh," he said quietly.

"You took my family's story, told it as if it was your own, and then *killed* my niece in it," she spat.

"And did you see the comments? People said that episode made them get clean, it made them feel less alone, it made them check into rehab, get through the grief of a loved one lost to heroin."

"Tell me, Matt," she said. "Did you ever actually do heroin?"

His eyes fell. "Like, once?"

"You are such a fucking fraud," she said. "You and Kim are the same person! It doesn't matter who you hurt, as long as it helps your *personal brand*," she said, disgusted. "You acted like you *liked* me just to, what, get into Loots Town?"

"I do like you!" he exclaimed. "But yes, I thought it'd be a good profile episode. It will be. I can cut you in on the profits." She laughed out loud. "Sasha, if you take that job, if you go undercover in Loots Town. We could do a deep-dive limited-run podcast and get it optioned as a movie. Easy," he slammed his sweaty fist on the bar in emphasis. She stared at it, the wet, weak, pale limb.

"Excuse me," a rough voice said. She turned to see a handsome Hispanic man with bloodshot eyes, swaying on his feet. "I am extremely fucked up right now, but did you just say you were in Loots Town?"

Matt looked around, she supposed in an effort to be furtive, but it just called more attention to them. "What do you know about it?" Sasha asked.

The guy smiled. His teeth were perfect. "My name is Jay, and I work for the White House."

Fifteen

Hunter Meadows Speaks Out from Prison (Retrieved from *The Washington Post*)

Hunter Meadows may be in the Caribbean, but he only sees an hour of sunshine per week.

The incarcerated real estate mogul has taken up working out and reading the Bible to fill the long hours in solitary, awaiting his trial for wire fraud, health code violations, and failure to provide habitable living spaces in his rental properties across the Eastern Seaboard.

"Prison makes you rethink everything," Hunter told the Washington Post via video conference. He was pallid with ropy muscles, and his amber eyes had turned hard. "Especially love."

While Meadows's ex-wife, Chloe Thibodeaux, is banned from social media, *Page Six* extensively covers her deluxe life in Russian exile, where she often accompanies Russian oligarchs to events and lives in a St. Petersburg palace formerly belonging to Russian nobility. When asked about his wife, who filed divorce papers ten days after Meadows was arrested in 2037, Meadows is clearly uncomfortable.

"I thought marriage was a partnership, thick and thin and all that. Call me old-fashioned but I thought Chloe would advocate for me, or at least take our children with her to safety." Meadows's children live with their grandparents in Rochester.

"I get that President Lopez wants to hold people accountable. I do, but Chloe gets to live in Russia? Getting around these new laws with a new company sponsored by Russian oligarchs. How is it that I'm in prison and she is the CEO of a start-up? She hasn't called me one time in prison after 13 years of marriage. 13 years! The father of her children." Mr. Meadows began to weep, softly, in his orange jumpsuit. "I pity her, really. I've been meditating and thinking back on my life. My biggest mistake was marrying someone so cold."

Chloe Thibodeaux was unavailable to comment on this article.

Want to read more? Sign up for Amazon Prime and make $50 in qualifying home decor purchases to finish this article!

SIXTEEN

July 16, 2038 | Санкт-Петербург, Россия

Chloe would *never* turn down an opportunity to comment. She poured a new glass of vodka and glared at the replies to the article. #FreeHunter was trending.

@ariesgirl46: Chloe Thibodeaux is a monster who deserted her family #LockHerUp and #FreeHunter.

@mattyglesias: First, Chloe advocates for violence against Kim, escapes prosecution, and doesn't speak up about the horrors of the American prison industrial complex. #FreeHunter

The article posited that Hunter is some kind of political prisoner with only a passing mention to his very real crimes as a multigenerational slumlord. No fact-checking whatsoever on his ridiculous story about trading cigarettes for Zoom time in Guantanamo Bay when the *Washington Post* obviously just scheduled a press call.

Chloe *did* like that Page Six was covering her lifestyle as luxurious, even if her "palace" was infested with cockroaches.

She shut her phone off and leaned back against the endlessly reupholstered couch. One thing that Chloe actually enjoyed about exile was that she no longer had sex with men. Her marriage to Hunter rested on an unspoken requirement that they had sex whenever, and wherever, he wanted to. Her modeling days were over when they got married and sex was her payment for his saving grace. If she was tired or uninterested, he would grow frustrated and assume she was having sex with somebody else and look through her phone. If she was stressed or busy, he would attach himself to her, wanting to spend "quality time" together (often in bed) watching television, squeezing her breasts until she turned to kiss him, just to get it over with.

Chloe may have loved Hunter at some point, but *he* got to stop trying and call it love while she had to hit the gym every day and never forget that sex was the cornerstone of marriage.

Who could blame him? Society fed a line that relationships die without constant companionship and physical intimacy. Hunter often cited studies claiming as much. So, she dutifully fulfilled her role as sexual meat puppet for the entirety of their marriage, ensured *his* desires were satisfied, did everything for him, until he was arrested and sent to Guantanamo Bay while she fled the country on a shipping barge, a favor from the Oligarch that Hunter set up. Hunter! She'd never said anything bad about him in the press. She agreed not to testify in his trial even though doing so would have provided her with immunity. As far as Chloe was concerned, she'd fulfilled her side of the bargain, it was Hunter who got himself arrested. He broke their marriage vows, not her. Without realizing it, she slammed the vodka glass so hard on the coffee table that it broke in her hand, cutting a deep gash into her palm.

"Shit," Chloe said, trying to staunch it with an eighteenth-century tapestry of Ivan the Terrible. A throat cleared behind her and Chloe spotted Sessa staring at her, shopping bag in hand.

"What?" Chloe said. Sessa held out the bag, an expensive one with a velvet cord. Chloe took it with her non-bleeding hand, letting the other one drip onto the hardwood floors. She fished out a folded note with her name on it rested on tissue paper.

"Chloe, please accompany me to dinner tonight" in neat cursive with the Oligarch's signature. She pawed through the tissue and discovered a tight, across-the-shoulder sweater dress from Balenciaga.

Chloe hated Balenciaga.

Seventeen

July 16, 2038 | Санкт-Петербург, Россия

The Oligarch grew up in Norilsk where his great grandfather was imprisoned in a gulag that had no fences because the unforgiving tundra was its fence. He played along the side of a thick, red river, bright and soupy from the mine runoff, creating a gash against the tundra. All of Siberia sat on a massive swath of volcanic rock. 250 million years ago there had been an "eruptive event" lasting two million years and culminating in the Great Dying, killing 96% of all marine species and 70% of all land species. The bones of these creatures liquified into fuel. The extended eruption created the deposits of nickel and palladium in Norilsk. Siberia was rich in death.

The Nganasan people knew too. The tribe held seances in the polar night, wild affairs where the soul communicated with the gods. The last shaman had a vision that a Russian god would defeat their shaman god and rule all of Siberia. He knew these things because he grew up near the blood river and the lake that never froze over next to the smelter. He knew these things because he grew up alongside the Nganasan. In the 90s, the Oligarch knew what needed to be done. All things must die to make money.

The Oligarch rented the entire restaurant out. Waiters stood at every corner with wine and caviar. He liked Chloe. She sipped vodka while he asked polite questions about her fake company. For an American, she had a Soviet work ethic, and he admired that. The Oligarch's shipments went in and out of American airspace with no questions. They all thought it was breast milk. Americans never questioned the stupidity of other Americans. If circumstances were different, he would hire Chloe to do something real. She believed the lie. She dedicated herself wholeheartedly to the cause of the lie. In another life, she would have made a wonderful gulag guard. He fantasized about Chloe beating him within an inch of his life.

"Sir?" Chloe said, politely, looking him directly in the eyes. He snapped back to attention. She tapped on the glossy business plan.

"You've done good work," he said. Chloe smiled, though there was something missing in her eyes. That determination. The belief. "You read your husband's article; I imagine?"

Chloe shrugged, though he could tell it bothered her. "We're all doing PR to stay rich."

"Precisely," the Oligarch said, pleased.

She raised her perfectly plucked eyebrows. He admired that she took the time to pluck her eyebrows now that she had no access to painless hair removal. She chose to suffer. She ate small bites and chewed slowly, thoughtfully. She never did anything halfway.

"You're going back to America," he said, carving into his steak and putting a bloody piece into his mouth.

"I'm not allowed to go back to America," Chloe said slowly.

"Well, not America," he said, chewing. "Loots Town."

"Loots Town," she said, trying out the words.

"No need to worry about commercial airports. You will never step foot on American soil on the way there," he said, appealing to her nature. "You're not poor."

"I'm needed here," she said. "With the company."

"There's no need to worry. Willem assures me of his protection."

"Willem," she repeated.

"Yes, he wants you back there. He paid handsomely for your safe arrival." Chloe said nothing. "You don't like Russia, right?" The Oligarch said. "Sessa says you always complain about the cold and how old the house is."

Chloe put down her fork and crossed her arms. "So, she *is* spying on me."

"Naturally," the Oligarch said, dunking a piece of steak into caviar and washing it down with wine.

"And now you're selling me to Willem?"

"Think of it as a transfer," the Oligarch said, waving his hand. "This is politics. The movement of people, money, things."

"You're not a politician," she said.

"All rich people are," the Oligarch said. "It's time you learned that."

Chloe stared at him.

He paused and patted her hand. "It'll be better for you there. Comfortable."

Eighteen

"Life is too short to pay rent lol."
— Willem Loots

September 15, 2038 | Loots Town

Sasha leaned against her balcony, looking down at the main boulevard of Loots Town. The sky dome was dimming for the sunset hour. An artist ran the sunset simulations, and they were always gorgeous in the typical orange and pinks as it faded into a brilliant live stream of Saturn from Loots's telescope in the sky. She heard laughter down below as a group of shirtless men played volleyball in one of the parks extending out onto a platform from the residences, creating shade for a sushi restaurant underneath. Everything in Loots Town had a dual purpose, existing in tandem with something else. Symbiosis, Loots called it.

Sasha was astonished at her own sense of well-being. She had never felt so at peace before. She could dedicate herself wholly and completely to her work with no distractions. How did people work at their jobs, work on themselves, pay bills, have a relationship, develop hobbies, and socialize all while maintaining sanity? In Loots Town, those worries floated into the automated sunset. She felt like she did in Los Angeles, like she was useful, a leader, building something. She missed that feeling so much.

"Sasha," Moore said. "It's time for you to go on." She took one last look at the sunset and walked back into her suite. Her living quarters were two rooms— a small bedroom, a large open plan living room and kitchen that opened up onto the balcony with a jacuzzi. She sat at the sleek white desk where her open LootsBook waited. A producer for CNNBC explained how her segment would work, but she was used to it from her brief fame after Kim. She smiled at the woman in New York City, her hair a mess, dark circles under her eyes. Sasha faintly remembered what it felt like to be that unhappy.

Two months ago, at the Chicken Ranch, Sasha and Jay made a plan. She would take the job at Loots Town and recommend Jay to Dima for the HVAC job. In exchange, Jay would ensure Maya got excellent (and free) care at the Walter Reed National Military Medical Center. She expected to be in and out within thirty days. Certainly before Maya went back to school. She did what Kenny, the teenaged CIA agent, told her to do and attached a bug to an electrical panel in her building's server room.

Then, they went radio silent.

Sasha knew that she should care about that. She knew she should find Jay, quit this job, and go back to Las Vegas but those feelings existed far away, in a foggy, forgotten corner of her brain. She could barely remember the interview conducted, she was so carefree and calm. Her work life before was punctuated by anxiety. What would Kim scream at her for that day? Mariko was a hands-off boss. Sasha took her earbuds out, picked up a tablet and pored over the media chatter about her segment. A clip was already going viral:

JEN PSAKI: I don't think it would be too farfetched to say that the general public is shocked you're living in Willem Loots's innovation zone, the richest man in the world, after your past with Kim Kardashian.

SASHA IVANOV: I have no regrets about blowing the whistle on Kim. The difference between Willem and people like Kim is that he's trying to build a better future for the world while Kim was trying to build her wealth portfolio, at the expense of human lives.

JEN PSAKI: What's it like in Loots Town?

SASHA IVANOV: It's beautiful. People are encouraged to follow their dreams. For the first time in my life, I'm encouraged to put myself first. Technology is miles ahead of America. The entire town is run on renewable energy and LootLink satellites in orbit from the nearby LootPort provide state-of-the-art, and free, telecommunications to residents. In fact, all utilities and rent in Loots Town are free. As long as you contribute to the wellbeing of the community, you are provided with whatever you want.

JEN PSAKI: That's exactly what unnamed U.S. intelligence officials are telling CNNBC.

Jen was practically salivating at the idea of Loots Town. A notification appeared from Mariko (whom Sasha still couldn't tell was human or not) that Jen had already applied for citizenship, a $2 million purchase of LootCoin, which had already gone through with an associated bump in the crypto currency's value. The first crypto that had the power of a thriving country behind it.

"You did great," Moore said, kindly, rubbing Sasha's back. "You looked so beautiful." She was still amped from the interview, her mind racing a mile a minute. She leaned into his knuckles as they worked through the knots in her back. "Let me make you tea," he said.

"You don't have to," she said but he was already at the apartment's granite kitchen island, heating tea, and measuring loose leaf green tea into a cup. She watched him. Moore was assigned as her "guide" to Loots Town right after she came back and took the job. While he didn't live in the apartment, he was with her wherever she went. He was easily the most attractive man she had ever met, and she had lived in L.A. for years, gone to parties peppered with celebrities, been waited on by wannabe actors with bodacious biceps. He had an accent, Brazilian perhaps, but he didn't talk much about where he was from. She could often see his chiseled six-pack as he reached his arms over his head during their yoga sessions. He styled his hair back, away from his face. He smiled easily, his jawline was defined and covered in a perennial five o'clock shadow. It was like they had built an android based on her ideal man. She was sure Moore was human —at least, pretty sure. He complimented her often, asked her questions about herself, made wonderful food, and ensured her days glided by.

NINETEEN

September 15, 2038 | Yurts Town

Sweat streaked across his safety goggles as he squeezed sealant, like toothpaste from the tube, to vacuum seal the ducts together. On the outskirts of Loots Town, among the strangely beautiful handmade yurts, he was far from the wasteful temperature-controlled town center. It was a desert, and here on the edges he really felt it. Hence the HVAC installation. The yurts were efficient both for living and constructing, tubing up the lumpy hovels on a dirt mountainside felt to Jay like he was installing central air for the Taliban.

It was the hardest he'd ever worked. Before this, he didn't even know what real work was. Not really.

Which is not to say it was mentally taxing. It wasn't. There was a kind of soothing repetition to it, actually. Though the yurts didn't have the typical crawl space or existing ductwork that he might have found installing a system in a traditional home, once he had figured out a method for running the tubing through drilled holes in the walls, the process had become mechanical. He became anonymous, unseen.

That was exactly the way Jay wanted it.

It had been two months since he pulled the SIM card from his phone and crushed it into dust with his heel on some Nevada highway. He had immediately felt a weight lift, a distinctly physical feeling, like a crane had raised a Mack truck off of his chest. He hadn't previously even given himself the time to consider the never-ending latent stress that came from being always on-call to the President of the United States. For the first time in his adult life that he could remember, he didn't have a direct line to some boss that could harass him in his pants pocket.

Now he answered to a whiteboard. He showed up every morning, bright and early, to a makeshift bungalow, temporary and utilitarian like a FEMA shelter, where they'd all get their assignments for their daily work and a protein shake to stay hydrated in the unrelenting desert heat. The board listed a location in Yurts Town and he hoofed it over there, finding the HVAC system, already delivered in a box, and he'd get to work drilling, routing, sealing, and running electricity. It was impersonal, anonymous. Jay had never even seen the foreman or whoever updated the whiteboard. He just arrived in the morning, every morning, he had yet to have a day off, alongside the other dusty sunburnt laborers and scanned the whiteboard for his assumed name: Pablo.

He had been cute with the fake name he'd given Kenny for his fake papers to enter Loots Town. *A little too cute*? he had worried at first. But he had been working anonymously and quietly for ten days now without any issue. What was more likely, that this migrant worker who showed up was a former aide to the President using the President's first name as a weird "fuck you," or that he was just one of the infinite number of Latino men named Pablo?

His disappearance from D.C. hadn't gone unnoticed, of course. As anonymous a profile as he had kept, the sudden disappearance of a senior advisor to the President couldn't go unremarked on by the press. Even on the closed LootsWeb curated internet, he was able to find articles about his disappearance, probably allowed because it made Pablo look bad. He was the subject of newly-formed conspiracy theories about the administration. #LopezBodyCount trended for a week straight, the crux of the conspiracy being that Pablo had carried out a secret execution of Jay at the behest of Kim Kardashian's attorneys. Jay knew his disappearance probably tore Pablo up inside.

Good. Fuck him.

Pablo could have called Jay himself to essentially fire him but instead he hid behind Lupe. As far as Jay was concerned, Pablo didn't deserve Jay's Beltway breakfast sandwich delivery.

Another face he saw on LootsWeb was Sasha. The former Kardashian whistleblower was now a major part of the PR organ for Loots Town. At the time, he thought they would be able to meet and compare notes but there was a structural caste system in Loots Town. Jay lived in Yurts Town. Sasha lived in Loots Town. The two never interacted.

Jay had infiltrated Loots Town to act as a spy. To put his own body on the line where Felix's unimpressive team had failed, in order to collect the necessary information about the evils he was sure were taking place so that he could re-emerge in D.C. with an airtight case for Loots's execution. He was going to pose as a laborer until he had the smoking gun and could return to his best friend in triumph.

It turned out espionage was a lot harder and more boring than it seemed in the movies. After installing some bugs in Yurts Town, nowhere near to discovering any smoking gun, he had spent the last two months installing HVAC systems. He was getting good at that at least.

He decided to duck his head low and lose himself in the work. To trust that if he were anonymous, diligent, and unseen enough that eventually some kind of evidence would produce itself. Rich whites always did and said fucked up shit in front of the help—he just had to commit to being the help long enough.

Twenty

LOOTS LOOP (retrieved from loop.loots.web)

Loots Loop™ is now open to residents.

Tunnel technology is the next generation of transportation. Why tunnels? Weatherproof with minimal climate impact, they move Loots Town residents in style. Tunnels are proven to completely fix traffic and, eventually, will unlock high-speed, luxury regional transit.

The average walk time between Maloti Dome and Maseru Dome (named for locations in Willem Loots's homeland of Lesotho) is thirty minutes. Loots Loop can do it in ninety seconds using Pegasus electric self-driving cars. The average wait time for a vehicle is 6.9 seconds.

The Loots Loop reduces traffic on the ground and reaffirms Loots Nation's net-zero carbon commitment as it grows.

The system is designed to transport over 5,000 people per hour. Passengers load into vehicles capable of holding three people and the car navigates six miles of tunnels underneath Loots Town to twelve different stations. Every day, individuals are hard at work to improve and expand the system. The potential of Loots Loop is unlimited.

Twenty-One

September 17, 2038 | Loots Town

Loots Loop was a nightmare.

The stations were beautiful, Sasha had to give him that. Neon lights accentuated the stylish curves of the Pegasus vehicles. Mounted screens played *Rick & Morty* and *Epic: The Willem Loots Story*, a major motion picture starring Timothée Chalamet as a (somewhat) young and feisty Willem Loots hustling in Silicon Valley.

The problem was the vehicles. There were too many of them. Passengers boarded and waited sometimes hours to travel a distance of a quarter mile, trapped underground in gridlock, locked in their cars with no way out. Prince Harry had a panic attack on one ride that lasted six hours. On rare occasions, the vehicles did make the trip in ninety seconds, by clipping the walls of the tunnel, hitting other cars, and in one case hitting a tunnel worker at eighty-five miles per hour.

Sasha and Moore stood staring at a line of vehicles stretching endlessly through the tunnels. A crowd of residents, curious at the "next generation of transportation" waited for hours to ride. Sasha did damage control, including offering Prince Harry and his family an all-expenses-paid trip to Real Tatooine to keep his experience hush-hush. They were just kinks! Every new technology has them! As Willem Loots says, optimistic and wrong is better than boring and right. The future at work!

Mariko approved a few hours of road closure so that Ashton Kutcher could ride the Loots Loop as intended. The self-driving cars were all parked off-site.

"What once was a half hour walk now takes seconds," the aging Ashton said into the camera, as he descended the escalator into the Loots Tower station. "That means more time with my family," his new young wife and baby joined him, "And less for my commute." Sasha wrote the words without knowing if Ashton Kutcher even had a job, and if that job had an office, and whether that office was even in Loots Tower. Everyone technically had a job "giving back to the community" in exchange for continued residence but Sasha knew that people like Ashton Kutcher, who paid in LootCoin to live and avoid taxes here, did jack shit.

Ashton, his child bride, and the gurgling baby waited exactly 6.9 seconds (she rehearsed it and timed it with Loots workers) for an elegant SUV to glide into the station. He got in and the car accelerated to 60 in 1.8 seconds (they replaced the engine of the car with a gas guzzling formula one prototype). Sasha watched it speed through the tunnels, hoping against hope that it did not explode. A racing team awaited Ashton at Maloti Dome station to ensure his safety and cool down the vehicle. It would be dismantled after this promotional video.

"The video is aspirational," Mariko told Sasha dismissively, "We'll get there soon." This "fake it 'til you make it" mentality was a core component to Loots's personal philosophy. He just called it "innovation" and "wonder" instead.

"Loots Town is reinventing transportation the way it reinvents every aspect of living– to make it meaningful, groundbreaking, and luxurious." Sasha said to the camera, her hair elegantly braided, her makeup perfect. She grinned until the director said cut. She then sighed, massaging her temples. The temperamental director, known for his off-kilter framing and inverted camera angles, had called for forty-five takes of her saying that one sentence. Grumbling after every single one.

"Are you okay?" Moore appeared by her side. She jumped. "LootsMaté?" he asked, holding out a bottle.

"In a second," she said in irritation. It had been a long day.

"It'll make you feel better," he urged. She relented and took the bottle before walking off. "Where are you going?" Moore called out nervously.

"The bathroom," she snapped without turning around. Sasha knew she shouldn't be mean to Moore, but Loop Hell had infected her mood.

A neon light directed her to the all-gender restrooms. She closed the door and peed, relishing the alone time. While Loots Town was luxurious and comfortable, it could also be claustrophobic. People were *always* around and the walls had a way of closing in around her.

As Sasha exited the bathroom and headed towards the station, she heard a high-pitched scream. Sasha froze. The station wasn't quite finished yet and the walls (with corners) were only halfway completed. She walked towards the sound. At the end of the hall, Sasha found a door. She stood on her tiptoes to see out of a grimy window. A massive hangar: likely positioned under Loots Tower. Workers were unloading something from a huge airplane. Men in fatigues yelled in Russian and moved crates marked with "FRESH BREASTMILK." *What the?* Sasha thought. Then someone tore open the box and pulled out some serious weaponry, a grenade launcher, M16s.

More crates were offloaded, each of them filled with guns, Kevlar vests, artillery shells, a fucking torpedo. Then, they opened a box and a girl stood inside. She was Maya's age, skinny, dirty and weeping, her hair in two braids. She kept screaming in Russian: Где я? Где я?

Where am I?

A hand closed over Sasha's shoulder and squeezed painfully.

"Lost, Ms. Ivanov?" Mariko said.

Twenty-Two

September 17, 2038 | Loots Town

Today was finally the day.

Chloe sat leaned back in a dental chair, her mouth opened wide as a heat lamp dried the whitening gel that had been slathered across her teeth. The dentist, a tan and healthy middle-aged man, sat nearby, tapping away at some game on his phone. An assistant had preceded his arrival, setting up the chair and all of his equipment for the doctor's house call. Chloe assumed, at least, that this was her house. It was where she had been placed in the months following her arrival at the dusty desert tarmac among the wooden boxes of breast milk.

Waiting for an opening in Willem Loots's busy schedule.

She wasn't complaining that much. She *did* live in a yurt, but it was outfitted with appealing modern furnishings and a very comfortable and expensive bed. There was a pool outside she could sit by for hours and anything she required was brought to her.

She did note that two security guards equipped with AKs were stationed at the yurt's entrance, always watching her.

She had resigned herself to her situation. She had been bought and sold. Three times. First, Hunter had bought her, then he sold her to the Oligarch, and the Oligarch had flipped her to Willem Loots. She realized that in the end she was just another real estate deal to these men. Another property they tired of and then sold to the highest bidder as a "fixer-upper with great potential."

The week had been dedicated to doing the "fixer-upping." A parade of professionals had been sent one by one to her yurt to tune her up. Day one: A technician had lasered off every follicle of hair not on the top of her head. Day two: A dermatologist froze and removed moles. Day three: A manicurist rounded and trimmed her finger and toenails. Day four: Bleach was applied to her asshole. At the end of each day, the stunning woman who had greeted her at the tarmac—whose name, she had learned, was Mariko—arrived for an inspection. She looked Chloe up and down like a judge at the Westminster Dog Show, the day's body perfection expert at her side, pointing out and requesting small changes or providing her approval. The asshole inspection had been the most degrading. While Chloe didn't exactly love being examined like a dog, she also couldn't deny she missed undergoing these procedures which had once been a constant, voluntary part of her life. So, she quietly submitted.

Chloe assumed this meant she was about to meet Willem.

The dentist swiveled the heat lamp away from her face and scrubbed the whitening goo from the inside of her mouth. He examined the color of her teeth. He seemed satisfied with his work, sent a text on his phone, and moments later Mariko stepped in for her daily inspection. She produced a color swatch from her small designer handbag and compared the swatch against Chloe's teeth. She examined them closely, squinting her eyes. Then, she curtly nodded. "This will do," she said, addressing the dentist. "A Pegasus is waiting outside to return you to Loots Tower." The dentist gathered a few of his supplies and headed for the yurt's exit.

Mariko pointed, gesturing for Chloe to stand up. Chloe dutifully did so, removing the dental smock and revealing a skintight slip underneath. Mariko gestured for her to do a turn, and Chloe did so, slowly. Mariko looked her up and down, carefully, referencing and taking down quick notes on a digital tablet. When Chloe finished her turn, Mariko gestured for her to do another. This felt like the most thorough examination Chloe had undergone thus far.

Finishing her second loop, Mariko stared at her with a piercing glare for an extended period of time. Finally, she broke the silence.

"Acceptable," she said simply with a quick nod. "Please make sure to get enough sleep tonight." She pulled two blue pills from her handbag. "If necessary, use these sleeping pills. Tomorrow, you will be introduced to Mr. Loots."

Twenty-Three

September 18, 2038 | Loots Town Border

Kenny was not getting paid enough for this. The desert, even in September, even at night, was scorching hot. He could already feel his future sunburn through the layers and layers of sunscreen he'd slathered on.

Loots Town was surrounded on all sides by a twenty-foot fence patrolled by hundreds of guards. Luckily Loots was giving the plebeians some PTO for an NFT art show. Kenny grew up with Monet, Rembrandt, all hanging in the halls of his mother's palatial estate in upstate New York. He took this job not because he hated the rich, but because Loots was so bad at it. The richest man in the world and his life was one big 69 joke.

He knew about the NFT gallery because of the backdoor he'd built into Loots's intranet. He needed more though. The intraweek gave him access to essentially public (within Loots Town, anyway) information, but nothing about the inner workings of the secret city. That's why he'd hiked a dozen miles through the desert, nearly dying of thirst, to plug his laptop into the server at a border outpost.

He tapped away on his laptop, thinking of the girl he would

purchase that night. Emily was nice. She held him as he cried softly. A glitch queen may do the trick though. He just wanted to pump away and not feel so guilty about it. It has been a long day. He sent a communique to Felix, snapped his laptop shut, and sighed at the thought of his long journey home. He didn't have much water left. He was going to request a Polaris. Bill the White House.

That's when someone put him in a headlock.

"Hello Jew Fuck," someone with heavily accented English said. "What are you up to?" A crack and the world went dark.

Twenty-Four

September 18, 2038 | Loots Town

It happened. A day off. *Two* days off. Jay was pretty sure it was the weekend, but Loots Town was such a closed circuit that the days had a way of losing meaning. Jay had a cot in a giant cavernous warehouse building—based on the blue accents on the exterior, he suspected it was formerly a Walmart. He gathered that many of the laborers who slept in the cots surrounding him had used their day off to go to the neighboring settlements in the Innovation Zone to pay to fuck anything that moved. Or, increasingly, to fuck things that didn't move. He'd overheard lurid tales in colorful Spanish about the orgasms—like nothing they had ever felt before—provided by what sounded like iPads plugged into USB pocket pussies.

The sex didn't interest Jay. Aside from the fact that he was unsure what his bunkmates would think of his sexual orientation, he had just lost the anxious urge for anonymous sex. Maybe he had just gotten his fill during his time in Washington. Or maybe it was the fact that, in D.C., he had used sex as a pressure release valve. Here, he had to admit to himself, he just wasn't feeling that kind of pressure, so he didn't need that kind of release.

Jay took a bus that sped through the congested tunnels of

Loots Town. He tried to get a good look around but the tunnels were dark and circuitous, and he lost count on how many turns the bus took. He arrived in a modern station and climbed the steps into one of the bubbles for the white-collar Loots residents. He walked the promenade aimlessly, enjoying the manufactured perfect weather. He stopped at a statue of Willem Loots with six-pack abs on what was supposed to be the surface of Mars. A placard read: *It would be cool to die on Mars with all my friends.* It was clear he was that special brand of narcissist who didn't think he needed a ghost writer.

Jay allowed himself to get lost in Loots Town, as he wasn't quite sure what he was looking for. He found himself at the foot of Loots Tower, the always-visible obsidian spike at the settlement's center. Most of the entryways were locked to anyone who didn't have the right keycard to scan. One door was open and flanked by beautiful women beckoning him in. A banner read: Loots Gallery! Open to All!

Jay climbed the stairs to The Loots Gallery of Non-Fungible Tokens. Inside, the walls were bright white and there was a calm in the air. An embrace of silence, save for a few comforting murmurs echoing like a rolling brook. From a podium, he was greeted by a welcoming docent. The middle-aged woman was dressed nicely in a professional blouse and khaki pants, but her skin was leathery from years in the sun, and her hair cut short, probably to remove a mess of impossible-to-tame dreads. This woman, Jay thought, was once homeless, and now was bright, happy, indoors. Useful. He felt a tinge of uncertainty. Maybe Loots wasn't up to something after all.

"Welcome to the grand opening of The Loots, a first of its kind gallery for non-fungible tokens," the docent said, her wide smile unwavering. "Do you have a reservation?"

Jay shook his head.

"That's fine, that's fine," the docent replied, tapping at the tablet affixed to the podium. "We can squeeze you in. Admission is free, thanks to the generosity of our benefactor, Mr. Loots. All of the art you're about to see is from his personal collection." She retrieved a tablet from the drawer and extended it to Jay. "Just remember to return your tablet when you're finished and enjoy your stay!"

Jay followed a path marked by arrow stickers on the ground to a wide white room. On the walls there were a series of square QR codes accompanied by small placards with text. Jay was confused momentarily but read an instructional card on a stand at the room's entrance. Using the tablet, he scanned the first blocky bar code and it was replaced on the tablet screen with a piece of digital art, artificially placed on the wall on the tablet with augmented reality. The digital piece was a pirate cat with an eyepatch in the retro 8-bit style of video games from the end of the previous century. Jay wasn't too impressed with the art, but he hoped at least that the artist—credited on the accompanying placard by their Reddit handle YubNubbers—was paid a lot of money for it. A timer ran down at the top of the tablet and the digital artwork disappeared from the screen, revealing again the QR code it had replaced that actually existed on the wall in reality.

The art was not very good. Much of it was in a similar 8-bit retro style—Loots had a fetish, it seemed to Jay, but perhaps not taste. He had a timed look at a purple cartoon ape rocketing over a looping space backdrop, a bowl of Japanese ramen with eyes peering back from the bottom of the bowl, and a classical portrait of George Washington with the head of a cat. There were lots of pieces that featured cats. Jay wasn't sure if this was a Loots preference, or just that cats were overrepresented in NFTs in general because of the internet's ever-enduring obsession with felines and oh-so-wacky random humor. Even the pieces that weren't in the 8-bit style had a lack of human artistic skill. With traditional art, Jay could more appreciate the technique of the artist on a structural level, like appreciating well-built architecture. With this digital art, there was an underlying awareness that much of the credit for technique had to be awarded to Adobe Creative Suite.

He spotted the firm dividing line between the haves and have-nots. Behind a velvet rope, there was a grand opening soiree available only to the Loots Town upper crust, the digital nomads and wealthy residents of Loots Town. Jay scanned their faces, keying up his resentment and seeing if he could lip-read anything incriminating.

No luck. All he could make out on their lips were gray smears of chicken liver pâté. Then someone pushed through the crowd. She looked directly at him.

It was Sasha.

She weaved past the velvet rope and sauntered directly to Jay. She stood next to him admiring a Nyan cat. "I have intel," she said in a low voice.

Jay raised an eyebrow in response.

Sasha was stone-faced for a moment, then rolled her eyes back, breaking into a big smile. "There are tons of weapons on the planes coming in," she said. "They're underneath us right now." Someone called her away and, just like that, she was gone.

Jay looked down at the polished tile floor.

Jay sat for the bumpy bus ride next to Fernando, a laborer of few words whose bunk back at the former Walmart was right next to Jay's. Fernando was characteristically silent for the bus ride. Jay didn't see him open his mouth once. Jay didn't know anything about this man, other than that, from the smell of pussy and Victoria's Secret perfume radiating from him, he'd spent his day off at the Chicken Ranch.

Jay spent the dark bus ride thinking about what he could do. Loots had weapons. Why else would he require weapons unless he was equipping an army? What was an HVAC guy, a spy so poor he had no way to contact anyone on the outside, supposed to do about weapon smuggling?

In the barracks (because that's what the old Walmart was, he realized), he showered, ate, and then he settled onto his bunk. He needed no blanket. The warmth of the crypto mining rig next door made it more than warm.

On the adjacent bunk, Fernando turned over and was now face-to-face with Jay. Only a few feet away. He opened his mouth, stuck out his tongue and Jay saw, with some confusion, that there was a small piece of paper on his tongue. Once the lights clicked off, Fernando removed the paper from his tongue and reached out his hand to Jay.

Jay unfolded the note, semi-translucent and smeared with saliva. He was shocked that he recognized the handwriting.

Felix.

"The wretched hive of scum and villainy. Tomorrow."

Jay hated that he got the reference. He'd be making the trek to Real Tatooine.

TWENTY-FIVE

September 17-18, 2038 | Loots Town

The wellbeing had died. In fact, the purpose and clarity she'd felt had deteriorated so rapidly she felt hungover, even though she hadn't drank more than a glass of wine here and there for months. She was even *proud of herself*.

Then she saw the guns and the girl.

Mariko had brought her to an antiseptic office called Loots Central Processing and left her in a windowless room for what felt like several hours until Dima came in. Sasha sprung up.

He looked tired and a little nervous. He twirled his blonde hair around a fingertip, a nervous tic of his. She wanted to scream at him, tell him they had to get out of here, but something on his face made her stop in her tracks. As did the camera in the corner with its red, blinking light.

"So, uh, hey," he said, sitting "Do you want something to drink?"

"Sure," she said, sliding back into the chair as he tossed her a LootsWater bottle. She uncapped it and took a long sip. She was surprised as the tension drained out of her and then took another look at the water bottle. When was the last time she drank or ate something that wasn't Loots branded?

"Um," he said, his face sweaty. "So Willem, well, Mariko I

guess, caught you in a restricted area. She wanted me to answer some questions for you."

"Am I in trouble?" Sasha asked.

"No, no," he said, "Curiosity is rewarded in Loots Town, under certain parameters."

"I was just going to the bathroom," she said.

"We know," he said. "I wanted to explain, um, what you saw." He ran his hand through his blonde hair. "So, the girls," he said. "They are refugees from the war in Ukraine." Russia's forever war that supposedly ended with President Lopez's peace deal. "Loots works with an orphanage there to find homes for those whose homes were destroyed by the shelling in the area." Sasha rolled this explanation over in her head. The Russian wars had been going on for so long that she didn't even think about them outside of election cycles when domestic problems in the United States were blamed on some despotic leader or another with access to 400 tons of wheat and oil in a county 5,000 miles away. "It's a humanitarian effort to provide them with top-of-the-line housing and schooling in Loots Town," he said. "I'll show you." He tapped a panel on the desk and a video feed appeared on one of the walls of happy children in a light Montessori-style classroom, 3D printing models of the universe. A teacher knelt beside them and pointed out different structures.

"What about the other stuff?" She said, turning away from the monitor.

Dima cleared his throat. "And the, uh, guns," he said. "As you're aware, we were attacked by a group of mercenaries over the summer." Sasha nodded. She wondered if he knew Alex the weed guy was one of them. "We just need to protect our people," he said, nodding to the feed of the classroom full of Ukrainian refugees.

Our people, she thought. Dima was a nationalist now?

Sasha examined Dima. He had a pleading look in his eye. From her past in PR, she understood that he was repeating talking points given to him by somebody else. He was always ill-at-ease with book reports in school. He was giving one now.

"Okay," she said. "That makes sense."

A look of relief spread across his face. "Okay, great," he said. "I wouldn't want you to think something bad is happening here. Mariko says you're doing awesome work. She wants you to keep it up. You know, for Maya."

Maya. It was like a gut punch. She hadn't thought of her niece in weeks. Hadn't called her in weeks. It always seemed secondary, below the surface, almost as if her anxiety about the girl had been sucked out of her. Mariko assured her a steady supply of insulin, and other support, was being sent to Olga.

Then, a coldness spread through her. Dima was threatening her. With Maya. She hugged her brother, told him they should get lunch sometime and that she would like to see the house. She needed to get out of there and find a way to warn Jay.

The NFT party had been a happy accident. Everyone had gotten a day off to see the show. When she saw Jay, she'd slipped away to tell him. The conversation with Jay had warranted a frown from Mariko.

"Why are you speaking to the help?" she'd asked. Some utopia. Sasha made something up about looking for hors d'oeuvres, which seemed to satisfy Mariko, though it was never clear with her mechanical eye and the unsettling stillness of her body (did she breathe? Sasha wasn't sure). She made the rounds and then went home, flopping onto the bed and turning on the TV. She flipped through the channels—LootsNews, a teen drama about Loots's wild teenage years, a feed of the rocket launches. The only things non-Loots produced were *Lost* and *Rick & Morty*, his favorite classic television shows. She turned it off. She missed America with its lawlessness and chaos and fury. At least it was *real*. She wasn't sure what Loots was doing but this dumb city was just a front for it.

Moore entered with a cup of tea. Her ever-present jailer.

She took a sip, and her rising anger melted into a relaxed

euphoria. Her shoulders drooped. She closed her eyes. Why was this feeling so familiar?

"What kind of tea is this?" she asked.

He laughed. "LootsGenmaicha," he said. He sat beside her and put his arm around her. She nuzzled into him, knowing somewhere in the back of her head that this wasn't okay, he was technically her employee. Wasn't he? It was hard to tell in Loots Town, then again it was hard to think beyond this moment, and he smelled like almonds.

"Where are you from, Moore?" She asked lazily, her eyes still closed. She felt him stiffen.

"Loots Town, of course," he said.

"But actually," she said.

"There is no before," he said, or she thought he said, and then he kissed her on the forehead. "You must be very tired. Let me take you to bed." She smiled at the thought of being in his strong arms, the feeling of his arms holding her up, the feeling of her silk sheets. She felt radiant.

She woke up in the middle of the night in a cold sweat. She realized what the feeling was. After all, she had been doing drugs long enough.

Ketamine.

Twenty-Six

September 18, 2038 | Loots Town

Willem's penthouse was gorgeous and ornate. It felt like she had stepped into a mansion even though she knew in her mind that she was on the top floor of Loots Tower. Mariko led her through the marble-floored entry foyer up a grand staircase. They passed a den with opulent leather chairs and beautiful wood shelves lined with books. Downstairs, she saw a massive dining table. They turned down a maze of hallways. As they approached a door, muffled sounds of gunshots and explosions came from the other side. Mariko opened it inward but did not enter. Standing in the hallway, she gestured for Chloe to go in. The room was uninviting, dark with murky hints of neon dancing inside. Chloe looked at Mariko, nervous. Mariko nodded, and Chloe felt somewhat comforted. She wasn't sure why she was comforted, she had no reason to believe Mariko had ever had her interests in mind. Maybe Stockholm Syndrome.

She stepped into the dark room.

Her eyes needed a moment to adjust, but after a bit, she saw at the other end of the room, in the darkness, shifting neon blues and greens in the shape of a chair. Bright light spilling from screens, too many screens, an overwhelming number of screens. Eight mounted high on the wall ahead of her, and two, partially obscured, lower, at desk-level. When her eyes fully adjusted, she saw that she was looking at the back of a sleek, sports car seat-like computer chair with an LED trim of shifting blues and greens. The screens mounted on the walls were all tuned to different video feeds which created a cacophony of overlapping noise. Three were feeds of cable news channels, two others were feeds of financial newscasts, one was a newscast from Chinese state television, one appeared to be a live-updating feed of the Reddit main page, and the last was playing an episode of *Rick & Morty*.

A voice cut in amidst the chaos, "Bro, I've got the flag, like, uhh... get the vehicle!" Chloe was suddenly aware of a human form sitting in the ornate computer chair. She stepped further into the room, unsure of how to get this person's attention, or what she was expected to do.

The person in the computer chair turned his head over his shoulder. Chloe recognized the face from the myriad LED bill-boards she had seen all over Loots Town, though here it was slightly fleshier, with hair plugs, and Botox pulling at the edge of his face so his beady dark eyes popped.

Willem Loots.

"Chloe Thibodeaux," he said. "Yeah, like... wow, holyshit. So nice to meet you. Come. Sit, sit." He gestured with his elbow, not taking his hands off his Xbox controller, at a chair to the side of his computer desk. Chloe took a seat. She looked at Willem in profile as his eyes flitted from screen to screen, ping-ponging between the eight mounted on the wall and the military video game on the computer screens on the desk. "Ohmygod, it's the first Pickle Rick episode. *Eheuheuheuheu.*" Chloe couldn't help but recoil at what she belatedly realized was laughter. "This is, like, the smartest show ever made. Have you seen it?"

Chloe shook her head. "I haven't."

"Fucking bitch idiot!" Loots exclaimed suddenly. He turned to Chloe and raised his eyebrows at her surprise. "Sorry, not you. The game." He turned back to the computer screen. "Don't get out of the Warthog with the flag, dude! Dude!" he screamed to the screen at his online teammates. But it was too late, a gravelly voice announced "Defeat!" from the screen. Loots pounded the

Xbox controller onto the desk. "Ohmygod, I can't believe you saw me lose. You must think I'm so lame. That's so cringe." He pounded the controller against his head over and over again. The outburst was nothing like Timothée Chalamet's suave Oscar-winning performance in *Epic: The Willem Loots Story*.

Chloe didn't know what to say, so she said nothing.

Loots turned and directed his full attention at her. "You look good, like, yeah, like, you look really good. Mariko did a great job." He pressed at his temple. "Mariko, you did a great job." He released the unseen subdermal button. "She's the best. Even though she's reaching the end of her shelf life, she gets me."

Chloe nodded, still not having quite gotten her bearings or the sense of how she was expected to act. "She's... great."

Chloe already lost his attention, his eyes were again dancing across the room's many screens. "Ohmygod, Nyan Coin is taking a shit. Kim, buy 300 WonkaCoin."

A speaker pulsed with a blue light and responded in Kim Kardashian's voice, "I'm placing that order now."

At Chloe's stunned reaction, he said: "I made it right after she croaked. RIP, truly. She was one of us," he said. "Although," he paused. "If it wasn't for her, we'd never have met. Walk with me?" He stood abruptly and walked away.

Chloe followed him out of the room. She was a hair taller than him. As they re-emerged into the light of the rest of the penthouse, she was able to get a better sense of Loots's appearance. A white giveaway Pegasus t-shirt adorned his lumpy torso, and below the waist he wore an ugly pair of Nike running shorts. On his feet he wore leather sandals that had too many straps. *With that many straps, why not just wear shoes?* She was struck with the thought that she could teach this man a lot about how to be wealthy. She kept pace with him as he speed-walked through the second-floor hallway.

"First of all, great work with the audition," he said. "UDDR was, like, such an absurd idea for a company. L.O.L." He actually said "L.O.L." out loud. Chloe felt a pang of betrayal. UDDR *was* a ridiculous idea, but it was a ridiculous idea that had made her feel in charge of her own life. "The whole thing was, like, actually a reference to *The Hangover*. Have you seen it?"

"It's been a while." How did this guy have so much time to watch movies?

Loots continued, as though her response didn't matter at all. "There's a scene where Heather Graham is, like, breastfeeding and it's totally random. And it gave me the idea to do this, like, totally random business basically as a joke. *Eheuheuheuheu*." He turned to her and made brief eye contact before breaking away quickly. "Yeah, but you are, like, really impressive. It was just supposed to be a joke, but, like, you got people to actually buy this stuff. We were just bottling like 15% breast milk filled out with goat milk and preservatives, but, yeah, your whole social media... thing made it almost, like, a real business." Chloe smiled, proud of herself. "But, yeah, you know, it served its purpose, like *you're here* now, so... I handed that off to an intern." He reached a heavy door and presented his eye to an ocular scanner to its left. The door slid open. "You wanna see something, like, really cool?" She stepped inside.

There was a large wall of CCTV screens, each showing a different section of Loots Town. A section of them displayed the village of yurts, laid out in precise rows and columns. Another group showed the LED lights of the colorful town center. Then a view from the office complexes at the foot of Loots Tower, then rows and rows of engineers in augmented reality glasses typing away at laptops. Then there were what appeared to be images from inside the residences at Loots Tower, taken surreptitiously. A doughy businessman laid in his tighty-whiteys on a large bed with two naked women at his side. Ashton Kutcher masturbating to a picture of himself. Some of the screens displayed what looked like mercenaries going through military drills. He quickly turned that one off.

It was overwhelming as Chloe tried to take it all in. The screens spanned the entire large wall in front of her and seemed to keep tabs on almost every square inch of Loots Town. Chloe turned to Willem, stunned. "Willem, this is..."

"Pretty rad, right?" he interjected, a childlike wide smile

across his face. "It's honestly, like, seriously, like, I'm a God here. Like, watch this." He pressed a button on a desktop console and spoke into a lens mounted on the wall. Chloe saw on one of the CCTVs that the image was being projected live onto one of the Town Center LEDs. "I am your God," Loots said into the lens. On screen, Chloe saw passersby in the town center cheer at the LED screen pronouncement. Loots released the console button and turned back to Chloe. "*Eheuheuheuheu*, it's, like, totally crazy." His eyes widened suddenly. "Oh my god, I almost forgot. You *have* to see this, it's, like, my prized possession." He reached into a drawer and retrieved an ornate gold handgun with an ivory handle. "This is, like, an antique. Belonged to my father. Used it to scare off the workers when they got too rowdy back when I was growing up in South Africa. It's so sick, it would be, like, paid DLC in a game."

The surreality of the moment steeled Chloe to finally ask what she had been wondering since she had arrived. "Willem, what am I doing here?"

Loots lowered himself into a swivel chair, his eyes once again flitted across the wall of screens. "Yeah... that's a good question. So, when Hunter sold you—Hunter's a *dick*, by the way, but that was a good move, it got him some working capital to get set up well in Guantanamo. But, when he sold you—I was like *shit*, the Oligarch! I've been trying to get a meeting with him for *ages*. So, I thought, why not Chloe? I really thought your posts about Kim were super L.O.L. But they were good positioning, too. Like, trying to straddle the line between obviously being a rich person but going viral over the execution. I thought it was, yeah, like, shrewd."

That hadn't been Chloe's intention, she was just posting and talking shit like usual, but she wasn't one to correct a compliment. "Thank you," she replied with a smile.

"And, you know, for me, it's like... it didn't work out with the pop star. It *really* didn't work out with the movie actress, *eheuheuheuheu*. So, I was thinking, like, after quickly rebranding you with UDDR, maybe the best move for me is a girlboss." He turned from the screens and looked into Chloe's eyes, for the first time. He saw she was not comprehending. "The idea is, like, for you and me to get married."

Chloe wished she was more shocked. She turned and looked at the screens, the totality of what had been created here in Loots Town. She turned back to the pasty, t-shirted billionaire who had just asked her to marry him. There was only one answer. She placed her hand on his.

"Sure."

A smile crawled across the face of Willem Loots. His eyes met Chloe's. "*Eheuheuheuheu.*"

Chloe's vision was obscured by a silk black blindfold Loots had asked her to wear. He had led her by the hand down hallways, giggling intermittently. She felt the downward movement of an elevator, then felt it come to a smooth stop, Loots pulling her by the hand from its door and forward. He led her down a tangle of hallways, and then came suddenly to a halt.

"We're here," he said, barely able to contain the childlike glee in his voice. "You can, ehh... take off your blindfold now."

Chloe raised the blindfold above her temples and down over her hair. In front of her was a door of brushed glass, exactly like the others that lined the rest of the hallway. Loots, grinning, tapped a keycard on the reader by the door. "Go ahead, open it," he said. Chloe reached out and tapped the indicator on the right side of the brushed glass. The door slid open.

Inside, she saw what the rest of the Loots Tower suites must have looked like. Smaller, of course, than Willem's penthouse, but still very nice. An open plan with high ceilings, a large living room just inside the door. Sitting on the large white sectional was a girl, probably 11 or 12 years old, eyes glued to an iPhone she was flicking. On the floor in front of a mounted 85-inch LED flatscreen was a boy, probably somewhere between 8 and 10, gripping a controller and staring intently at a game of Fortnite on the big screen.

Chloe was perplexed for a moment, unable to quite place

where she knew these two from. Then, with a sudden, sickening feeling, realized: These were her children. It had been a few years since she had seen them—and, honestly, she hadn't seen them too much before then, with her constant staff of nannies and tutors—but she was certain, these two human beings had come out of a surrogate Hunter paid.

"Connor? Helena?" she managed to stammer, stunned.

Helena frowned but didn't look up from her iPhone. "Mom? I thought you were in Russia. Like, forever." Connor stayed focused on his Fortnite match. It was unclear if he had even registered that his mother was there.

Chloe turned to Willem, aghast. He was not adept enough at social cues to read her expression. "Isn't it awesome?" he said, ecstatic. "I had them brought here, to, like, surprise you." He took her hand in his. "We can raise them here, together, and have *tons* more. I have, like, a bunch of random kids already, too. We gotta keep the birth rate up!"

Chloe turned from Willem back to her children who had barely acknowledged her appearance. "Willem," she said, through gritted teeth, "this was so, so sweet of you."

Chloe sat at one end of the massive dining table in Willem's penthouse, Willem sat, preposterously, at the head at the other end. Helena and Connor sat midway between them, opposite each other. It was a ludicrous use of the space. Helena still poked through her phone, TikTok audio occasionally playing from its speakers. Connor had switched to Fortnite mobile, his nose nearly pressed against the glass screen. Willem had asked them all to dinner, their first (he giggled) as a family.

Mariko emerged from a doorway, holding a tray on which sat four tall glasses. She distributed one glass to each of the happy family members. Chloe peered over the lid of the glass at the unappetizing gray sludge inside.

"Have you ever had this?" Willem asked exuberantly. "It's called Soylent Plus Kratom, and it's awesome. I used to eat Hot

Pockets for, like, every meal. Not good. *Eheuheuheu*. But I found out about this on Reddit, and it's much better. It's got, like, all the nutrients you need, and it's so much more efficient than the time it takes to eat a full meal." He took a long swig of the thick paste, then smacked his lips. "Try it!"

Chloe thought again that she could teach this man so much about being wealthy. Hesitantly, she took a small sip from her glass. It tasted like it looked—repugnant. She forced a slight smile and nodded to Willem.

"Yuck! Tastes like shit!" Connor cried out, mock gagging at his sip. "Fucking foul, L.O.L." He also said ""L.O.L." out loud, Chloe noted with a cringe.

Helena pushed her glass away, turning up her nose at it. "I don't put anything in my body without knowing how many carbs it has." *Good girl*, thought Chloe.

Connor looked to Mariko with a pleading expression. "Can we go? This is boring!"

Almost too quickly, Chloe responded "Yes." Mariko gave a nod of confirmation. In a flash, the kids bolted from the table.

Willem watched them go, with a chuckle. "They're great kids," he said.

"If you say so," Chloe responded.

"When we've finished our meal, I thought I might ask you for a dance," Willem said. "M'lady."

Chloe was disarmed. Despite how weird he was about *everything*, maybe Willem was sweet. Sweeter than the father of her children, anyway, who had sold her for, presumably, a flatscreen TV in his cell. Maybe she could get used to this odd little internet weirdo billionaire. Maybe, if she tried hard enough, she could even learn to love him.

"That would be nice," she replied with a smile, then tried to suppress her gag reflex as she forced down more of the flavorless sludge.

A jaunty and, to Chloe's ears, irritating song with scientific facts about the sun wailed from the booming sound system. Willem swung his arms and shook his hair, rhythmless, to the up-tempo nerd rock. Chloe had never even heard music like this and even hearing it made her feel vaguely embarrassed. But she endeavored to do her best to dance alongside Willem (not *with* him, not really, he was in his own world) in the marble-floored ballroom. She felt like a carnival-mirror version of Belle, a pasty man-child her Beast. Willem gripped her shoulders, looking in her eyes. Willem mouthed along something about the sun smashing atoms with the deeper-voiced singer during the song's breakdown. Chloe forced a smile, shaking her hair and, unsure of what else to do, pushed out a "Woo!" Willem's eyes widened, and he gave her a sudden closed-mouth peck on the lips.

He poured them a pair of whiskeys, straight, and sang along in harmony with a sea shanty, raising his glass in the air as he did, while Chloe mostly just sipped her whiskey and watched. He pulled what looked like a small asthma inhaler from a pocket in his basketball shorts. "Care for some ketamine?" he asked.

"I've never had any," Chloe responded.

"Oh, yes you have," Willem replied, puffing from the inhaler. "We put it in all our products. Turns out people are, like, docile if they're high all the time."

When in Rome, she thought, and took it and took a puff of the inhaler.

The K gave her a lightness and exuberance that almost made her forget that she was dancing with Willem along to a voice that sounded like text-to-speech. Willem giggled with glee as the autotuned voice crooned about apertures and science. Chloe couldn't see why Willem thought it was funny.

Willem, clearly also feeling the K, now danced close to Chloe, cheek to cheek. She felt the warmth from his fleshy, pockmarked face.

"Would you like, *eheuheuheuheu*," he said, not finishing the thought. They danced together to the odd song for another moment. Then Willem spat it out. "Would you like, um, to come to bed with me?"

Chloe had the feeling that maybe she was just another toy for this man, like his computers and his rockets and his self-driving cars. She also felt that this man was weak and malleable, and that she might be able to mold him right around her finger.

She looked in his eyes, smiled, and nodded.

He led her by the hand out to the hallway as the bizarre robot voice continued to sing about doing science and being alive.

Chloe lay on her back on top of the comforter on the massive bed in Willem's stately bedroom. She had donned a wig of short blue hair and a skin-tight white bodysuit—so skin-tight that it must have been created for her exact measurements. Willem had told her he was having her dressed as Rei from an anime called Ava... something. Chloe didn't know about that kind of nerd shit.

"Unzip the front," instructed Willem, between heavy breaths. He stood hunched at the foot of the bed, masturbating as he watched. Still wearing his white t-shirt, basketball shorts out of Chloe's view at his ankles. His eyes flitted between Chloe and a pair of tablets he balanced at the foot of the bed, loudly playing porn videos. "Play with your, um, play with your boobs," Willem grunted.

Chloe did so, unzipping the front of the bodysuit to pull out her pert breasts, fondling them. She focused beyond Willem, so that he would think she was still looking at him and she wouldn't have to suppress laughter at this billionaire chimp jacking off to her. Behind him was a wall-mounted neon sign of the number 42. It was the only thing that could be classified as artwork displayed in his bedroom. Chloe didn't know what it meant and didn't really care. *Probably from some fucking cartoon*, she thought.

"Great, unh, that's great, yeah, like. You look perfect," Willem grunted, increasing the intensity of his right fist pumping his member. "Mariko did a really great job." With his free hand, he pressed the subdermal button on his temple. “Mariko, excellent job on the Evangelion cosplay,” he said without missing a beat.

Chloe couldn't help but recoil, but caught herself and transformed it into a fake moan of ecstasy. “Ooh, I'm glad you like it, baby.”

“Take it, take it off,” Willem continued, short of breath. “Show me, *eheuheuheuheu*, show me your butt.”

Ignoring how infantile his dirty talk was, Chloe peeled the body suit completely off, and turned over, presenting herself on all fours. She prepared herself mentally for the moment of truth, expecting that now would be when the doughy man-child would enter her.

But the moment didn't come. Willem just kept pumping away at the foot of the bed. “That's good, yeah. That's really good. Now... turn back over. Play with yourself.”

Chloe flipped herself, and proceeded to mush her fingers around her vagina. She forced a few moans and focused on the wall behind Willem. It worked for Willem, his eyes now rapidly switching between Chloe and the porn on his tablet screens. “Oh my god, yes, yes, yessss!” Willem moaned as he sprayed on his Egyptian cotton comforter.

He climbed onto the bed and pulled the covers over himself and Chloe. He nuzzled into her neck.

“That was, like, incredible. Was it, um, was it good for you?” he asked.

“Oh, yeah, baby,” she responded. She wasn't even lying. While she couldn't say she had gotten any sexual pleasure from the experience, it was preferable to her lifetime of disgusting men pumping away on top of her and sweating all over her.

Willem mumbled “You're perfect” as he drifted into a post-nut slumber. Chloe closed her eyes.

She saw the afterimage of the number 42 burned into her retina.

Chloe stood on the penthouse deck as the desert sun rose, casting scarlet hues over Loots Town below. Las Vegas poked its head out from behind the mountains. She sipped from a glass of LootsYerbaMaté soda. It was the closest thing to coffee she could find in the kitchen. Her vision was sharp. Her brain hummed, moving faster than her body did. He had told her the truth. There were definitely drugs in this thing. She took in the totality of Loots Town, its full splendor. The neat rows of yurts. The white, veiny domes. Warehouses. An airstrip. A tall rocket perched on top of a launch pad. Did everything have to look like a dick with this guy? Willem seemed strange to her—like no man she had ever met before. But maybe he was a man for this age. He had built all this, *actually* built it. All Hunter had ever done was use his dad's money to screw over poor renters with buildings he'd bought that someone else had built half a century ago. Willem was a builder, a big ideas man who had the means and the force of will to execute those ideas. And, not for nothing, he seemed already incredibly smitten with her.

A glass door slid open behind her and Willem emerged, a neon-green plastic bottle of Mountain Dew in his hand. He stepped to her side and joined her in looking out over his creation. He squeezed one boob then giggled.

Chloe turned to him. "You know, what you've made here," she said, "it's really incredible."

"Yeah, you know, I'm, like, really proud of it," he replied, meeting her gaze. "But this is just the start. This is, like, the beta test."

Chloe raised an eyebrow. He was planning more than *this*?

Willem's eyes sparkled. "The real plan is Loots *Nation*," he said, taking her hand in his. "With you as my First Lady."

Chloe took this in, with a nod. She liked the sound of it. She looked back out over the Town, her mind now racing with the possibilities of his full plan enacted. Mariko broke her reverie.

"Willem," she said. "We have a problem."

Twenty-Seven

September 19, 2038 | Washington, D.C.

Pablo missed Jay. Being the President was lonely work, which was surprising given how often he was surrounded by people and noise. Being nominally the most powerful person in the country created a distance with just about everyone in it. By virtue of his position, people were either in awe of him, scared of him, wanted something from him, or outright hated him. Even his relationship with his family had been changed, probably irreversibly, by the job. The First Lady was exhausted by her jam-packed schedule of busy-work, her office over-scheduling her with the "Let's Get Reading" program, a nice sounding but impossible goal to get kids excited about reading again. His daughters would probably never forgive him for thrusting them into the national spotlight during their unfortunate teenage acne years. His son basically lived in his VR machine. Jay had kept their family together in a way. He was the one constant in their overturned lives. Now he was gone too. Because Pablo had let him down.

Pablo had dispatched the Secret Service to look for Jay but they came back with no leads. He'd finally gotten the opportunity to schedule a speech in Las Vegas in a few days, hoping it would draw him out, but he had to try one last thing.

"Mr. President, Juan Betteta is on the line." Pablo's assistant said. He picked up the receiver.

"Juan," he said, mustering as much enthusiasm and warmth as he could. "How is it going?"

"Great, Mr. President," he said. Pablo could hear shuffling and whispers on Juan's end. He was on speaker phone. "What can I do for you?"

"Jay went to Las Vegas a few months ago and disappeared. I was wondering if you had talked to him. I know you live out that way."

"You're calling about Jay?" he said dismissively, somehow critically.

"I just told you he's literally disappeared," Pablo's temper flared.

"I mean, no, I haven't spoken with him," Juan said. "I'm sure he's fine. The last time I spoke to him was to congratulate him on his new post and let him in on some real-world perspectives on the pharmaceutical world. The crackdown on stock buybacks makes sense for a lot of companies, but for healthcare, limiting that tool is dangerous to public health. Voting rights, preserving valuation, and having greater control of our financial statements help keep our company equipped to cure cancer."

"Where is that cure for cancer?" Pablo asked.

"We already have several drugs up for FDA authorization that, while not curing cancer, control the symptoms and keep people alive."

"A pill a day keeps the cancer away," Pablo said.

"Exactly! I knew you would understand. You're a sensible man. We're just trying to keep Americans healthy."

Pablo laughed. "Most of your R&D budgets are spent on suppressing affordable generic competition instead of curing cancer, so no. I don't think you're trying to keep Americans healthy, and I think you're a cocksucker who cares less about his own son than his yearly bonus and country club membership."

"I care about Jay," he said. "I know my boy would understand where I'm coming from. I'm just—"

"Your boy is pushing 40. He's a man now, a better one than

you ever were. The fucking gall. You should be ashamed of yourself," Pablo slammed the receiver down, knowing he'd done a potentially bad thing, but not really caring. A few minutes later, Lupe burst in, staring down at her iPad as she walked. She had an amazing ability to navigate the world with her eyes glued to her feed. Lupe cried that someone had taken a video of the phone call that Pablo had said the word "cocksucker" on.

"We have to issue a statement apologizing and condemning homophobia."

"He *is* a cocksucker," Pablo said. He was very tired. "Retweet the video and say that. A deadbeat dad and Big Pharma cocksucker."

"Polling shows—" Lupe started on another rehearsed speech. As she spoke, Pablo realized that she played him, for his need to be well liked, even while he was executing rich people and upending the system. He had this pathetic need to be liked. He'd had it his entire life. In high school, it was the football team and now, it was simply the vagaries of polling. "Are you listening to anything I'm saying?" she huffed.

"No," he said.

Her eyes lit up with fury, then quickly melted into composure. "You miss Jay," she said.

Pablo did. How did anybody navigate the presidency with no friends? She sighed. "I'll go to Las Vegas ahead of you and ask around. We'll smoke him out." She typed something into her iPad. "Just don't say cocksucker again while I'm gone," and strode out of the room.

Twenty-Eight

September 19, 2038 | Disney-Warner's Real Tatooine

A group of stormtroopers were standing at either side of the speeder track and Jay's speeder slowed to a halt. One of the stormtroopers approached the speeder. "How long have you had these droids?"

Jay rolled his eyes. He was not in the mood to play along with this. "Just skip it. I'm not interested," he said.

"Let me see your identification," the trooper responded. Jay gave him the middle finger. The trooper didn't react at all. The recreation was impressive, but his head pounded and the wind was strong today. Jay watched as a prop droid buzzed through the air.

The trooper sighed. "You can go about your business. Move along. Move along."

The speeder jerked back into action and progressed further along the track. Despite his mood, Jay felt a little guilty for how he'd treated the trooper. He was just doing his job, after all. He was just another minimum wage Disney slave who probably slept in his car at night just to bake in a heavy, plastic suit by day. Jay craned his head over his shoulder for a look at the speeder behind him, and he saw a group of large, sunburned adults all say in unison, "These are not the droids you're looking for," laughing and taking selfies with the stormtroopers on their phones.

The speeder reached the end of its track and the door slid open, Jay stepped out into the heart of Mos Eisley. He made his way through the throngs of adults taking pictures and gawking in awe (it was all adults here, Jay hadn't seen even one kid). Felix hadn't told him exactly where to go, but he knew intuitively exactly where to go. He headed for the curved entry of the Mos Eisley cantina.

The cantina was faithfully recreated except for the blinding lights, which did not agree with his splitting headache, and a soda machine that scanned an embedded chip at the bottom of the cup so people were unable to get free Mountain Dew refills. He squinted and glanced around, noting all the aliens he expected to see from the old movie scene which had been imprinted on his brain from the dozens of times he'd watched the Star Wars Special Edition Blu-ray as a loser teenager. Pablo used to come over and watch with him. An act of pity from the older, cooler family friend for a loser teenager with no dad, but then again he worshiped the guy. Pablo was his only friend, really. Jay was painfully shy in high school, still struggling with his sexual identity, and way too into Hot Topic.

A flat-headed alien with yellow eyes bobbed its head back and forth, a gray-furred beast with four black beady eyes scratched its chin next to the one with the massive cranium and the mouth that looked like a vagina. The one that looked like a dinosaur in a beanie slurped at a plate of spaghetti with bugs in it. *Wasn't it smoking some kind of vape in the original*? Jay thought, noting the Disneyfication of the bar: the erasing of the past while at the same time reinforcing nostalgia as the predominant form of pleasure in this world.

"Hey!" called out the bartender from the bar, pointing in Jay's direction at the entrance. The bartender was another of the minimum-wage cast members. He kind of resembled the bartender from the movie, with a prosthetic scar and flat rubber nose, but Jay could tell from his tenor that he had probably been in a high school theater program earlier this year. "We don't serve their kind here," the bartender continued, waving his finger around theatrically.

Jay arched an eyebrow. "Mexicans?" he responded.

The bartender lowered his eyes, bashfully. "No, uhh... *their* kind," he said, nervously. He nodded to Jay's left.

Jay looked to his side and found an animatronic C-3PO. Jay realized this was another of the scripted "experiences." A couple with nose rings glared at him, furious at his refusal to play along with the scripted interactions. He was ruining their immersion! Jay scoffed. Would real Mos Eisley cantina goers be wearing t-shirts with Goofy as Watto, or with the name "Darth Vader" in the Iron Maiden font?

He knew exactly where to find Felix.

In a booth in the back corner of the bar, seated next to an animatronic Chewbacca, he found Felix, drumming a finger on the table nervously.

Jay sidled into the seat in the booth across from him. "We couldn't have met somewhere that didn't cost me a $400 entry fee?"

"This is the only place I know we're not being watched," Felix said. Jay looked up at the dozens of cameras littering the ceiling, watching their every move, listening to their conversations to serve relevant ads to the console attached to their table. A new ad materialized across the screen, "The Naboo experience: privacy, seclusion, and beauty. Perfect for couples of any age."

Felix followed Jay's gaze. "Watched by *him*," he said.

"What happened?" Jay asked, wishing he would get to the point. He wanted to go back to his cot and lie down.

"You need to get out of Loots Town," Felix said. "Sasha, too. They know."

"What do you mean, they know?"

"Kenny," Felix said. "They got him."

"Is he alive?"

"When Auntie asked me to do this," Felix said, "I thought everyone would be safe. I don't think she knew what he was capable of. She is constantly underestimating people. Donald

Trump, Pablo Lopez, and now Willem Loots. She thinks that parlor tricks can knock people off kilter, and reestablish the slow, incremental change of voting for the party you hate least every November, or better yet, not voting at all."

"Why are you telling me this?"

Felix pulled out his phone and pulled up a video. Kenny sat in a windowless room, glassy eyed. He looked directly at the camera. "Loots Town is much more technologically advanced than we ever thought. The government is no match. I wish I had never tried to hack in. I wish I had never come here. Felix, don't let anybody come here." A few men behind the camera sniggered. Kenny winced, covered in sweat. Jay noticed that the camera only captured the top half of his body. Who knew what Loots and his men had done to the rest of him.

"He's just a kid," Felix said, then shook the thought from his head. "It's only a matter of time before Loots finds out about you and Sasha. You have to get out. I made this card for you. It should give you security access. Kenny's last gift to us. I'll have a team ready to extract you tonight, outside the eSports arena." Jay had never been to that part of Loots Town, though he'd seen the massive orb of it working in Yurts Town. It was supposed to be the biggest eSports arena in the world.

"Why should I trust you?" he asked.

"You really don't have a choice," Felix said.

Before Jay could respond, he heard: "Oonta goota, Solo?" Jay turned over his shoulder to find a green alien with black eyes, two small antennae with a face tapering into something like a small anteater trunk.

"Sorry to interrupt." A Disney employee quietly appeared at the side of the table, clad in a pastel-blue button down and clutching a tablet, looking, as most Disney employees did, like a member of the Sea Org. "We just wanted to inform you that your reservation for Han Solo's booth has expired." Jay noticed a group of tourists, nearly drooling in anticipation for their reserved time in Han Solo's famous booth, over the employee's shoulder. "Shoot the gun unless you'd like to extend your reservation," the Disney employee added, tapping at the tablet, "Credit only."

"We're done," Felix said, shooting the gun at the alien in the face, causing the animatronic to chime like a slot machine. He slid out of the booth. "Midnight," Felix said, and then disappeared into the crowd of nerds.

Twenty-Nine

September 20, 2038 | Loots Town

Sasha picked up her phone and dialed Maya's number, leaving her breakfast abandoned for the moment. She had called earlier in the morning. After a few rings, Maya picked up.

"Hi Mouse!" Sasha said brightly. A nickname she had not used in a long time. "How are you?"

Maya stared at her. "I'm fine," she said.

"Any problems with the insulin?" Sasha was sweating.

"It keeps coming in unmarked packages if that's what you're asking," Maya said. "Listen, are you ever coming back?"

"Of course," Sasha said. "I've just been very busy at work."

"Yeah, I saw you on TV," Maya said, bitterly. "So did all the kids at school. They said you're in a cult now."

"It's not a cult," Sasha said, though she wasn't so sure anymore. "It's just another way of living."

"You've disappeared with Daddy then? Is he okay?"

"I'm sure he's fine," Sasha said.

"You don't even know?" Maya exclaimed.

"We're both very busy!" Sasha said, her head beginning to pound.

"Well, I'm sorry to interject with some reality but Aunt Olga went to Sam's Town last week and hasn't come back. My teachers are beginning to ask questions."

"What?" Sasha said.

"It's okay, I guess I'll figure it out on my own. A ten-year-old paying rent! Have fun in

your creepy cult where all your dreams are finally coming true!"

"Maya," Sasha said, but she had already hung up. Sasha stared at the screen of her LootsPhone. Everything from her old life was gone and replaced with a gigantic "L" for Willem Loots. The mug on her side table, her cell phone, her tablet, the gigantic screen facing her bed, Moore's shirt as he knocked and eased open the door.

"Is everything okay?" She looked up, expecting to see his brow knitted together in concern. Instead, it was fear.

She locked her phone and set it aside. "Everything is perfect," she said, cheerfully.

"There is a worker here to see you," he said. He pushed open the door to reveal Jay, his eyes downcast, in a worker's blue jumpsuit with a toolbox in his hand. A dusty baseball cap covered his head.

"Miss," he mumbled. "I have to show you something. On the balcony. It's about the jacuzzi."

"Of course," she said, ignoring Moore's suspicious glance. She slid by him and walked outside, Jay followed behind her. She closed the door behind them.

"What the fuck are you doing here? How did you get here?" Sasha knew workers only had limited access to the domes.

Jay looked around, presumably scanning for a listening device, before guiding her closer to the edge of the balcony and the Infinity Jacuzzi. He looked around again, as if suddenly noticing his opulent surroundings.

"Wow, you really have it much better than I do," he said. He craned his head over to look back at Moore who watched them from behind the sliding door. "Who is the guy?"

"He's my servant, I think," Sasha said. She really didn't know.

"He's your servant?" Jay asked. "They give you servants?"

"I really don't know what else to call him, he does servant stuff."

"Do you have sex with him? He's really hot."

"Jesus, Jay, no!" Sasha said. "Focus, please!"

"Sorry," he said, rubbing his head. "Brain fog."

"Had a YerbaMaté lately?" she asked. He furrowed his brow in confusion.

"Not today, I woke up before the others to get to you."

"Then you missed your daily ketamine dose."

A realization dawned on Jay's face. "Shit," he said.

"I need to get out of here," she said. "They threatened my niece."

"Okay, okay," he said. "I know. I got word from Felix. We're compromised. Kenny got pinched."

"The computer kid?"

"Yeah," Jay said.

Sasha cursed under her breath. "He'll break within six hours of separation from his porn VR rig."

"I know." Jay ducked to open a panel on the jacuzzi. She glanced at Moore before leaning to examine it.

"Do they know about us?" she asked in a low voice.

"I'm not sure what they know, but I have a plan to get us out." He screwed open the panel and shuffled some wiring around.

"What is it?"

"Can you get to the eSports stadium at midnight?" He closed the panel and screwed it back deftly.

"Midnight, are you fucking kidding me?" Sasha exclaimed. Her heart began to race. She needed permission to leave the fucking *dome* she lived in. The eSports stadium was a construction site! "I have no fucking clue!"

Before Jay could respond, Moore opened the door. "Are you done?" he asked anxiously.

"Remember to turn it off when you're done, miss, we've been having leaks across town," Jay said and then left, taking a last look at Moore's ass before he vanished.

Sasha sighed. They were such shitty spies.

Thirty

September 20, 2038 | Loots Town

Moore had been listening to Sasha's conversation through his earpiece, concealing the alarm he felt throughout his body. He had a chip monitoring his levels and if it registered panic, a LootsWellness professional would check in on them, on the feed he was listening to, and when they found out that he had lost control of his charge, he would have to go back to the mine.

He would not go back to the mine.

Moore pulled out his phone and checked his Sasha app to see if anybody was listening in. Usually, he would hear a click in the feed, and the app would tell him with certainty if security section was doing a cursory scan.

He exhaled when he found the line was clean. The only option was to help Sasha. Maybe she could help him leave too.

Moore had left Brazil for a high-paying construction job that was supposed to last six months. He needed money to send back to his wife and daughter. That was two years ago. He had not been paid and spent most of his time working in the mines, living in a camp full of other prisoners. Moore checked his watch. He needed to get Sasha off the grid. Security section didn't know anything yet. That could change at any moment.

Moore typed up a text message on his watch. After he had gotten rid of the worker, he joined Sasha on the balcony.

The sky dissolved into the launchpad 20 miles away.

"These are happening more often these days," Sasha said offhandedly to Moore, gazing up at the countdown. As the rocket lifted up, the ground shook, and the fake sky pixelated slightly, revealing its actuality as a dark, veiny cave.

Moore perspired. "I don't think any more than usual," he said. In fact, it was much more than usual and the gossip amongst the other guides indicated that Willem was planning something. Not every launch was televised, they said, because not every launch was successful and Loots Town Resident Guide SOP rule 69.3 was to indicate that everything in Loots Town was successful.

"They are quite striking though," he said.

"Quite," she said.

"Ready to go?" he asked.

"Of course," she said in an even tone of voice. Sasha was cool under pressure. She would need that today.

Thirty-One

September 20, 2038 | Loots Town

It was good that the bird was on fire.

Chloe directed the chef to stuff the peacock with gruyere cheese and put a sparkler in its mouth that shot flames for the delight of her guests. The bird's green and blue train fanned out around it. Chloe looked the bird in the eyes, pleased that it was dead. When she saw the bird wandering around the main avenue of Loots Town, delighting guests and residents alike, she directed Mariko to capture the bird and have it slaughtered.

"Are peacocks a delicacy?" Mariko asked, taken aback.

"I don't care," Chloe said. She harbored a deep-seated hatred for peacocks. She didn't like things that had the sole purpose of being beautiful. It was better to slaughter them. She thought it would please Willem and the former royals. She was right. They clapped with joy as a servant carved a breast from the fiery bird.

"That is a fine peacock," a former English prince said. When the English monarchy was dissolved, Loots Town embraced them, former titles and all, as long as they paid the extravagant resident fee. In a way, despite all of its pandering towards innovation and futurism, Loots Town was about murdering the present in favor of the past—a more gilded time when the Earth was full of treasures and oil and the caste system firmly intact.

Willem squeezed her hand then tilted his head to the side, a signal from his earpiece. He excused himself. Once he had left, the bitchy duchess turned to Chloe.

"I'm sure you've heard the news," she purred. Chloe snapped her fingers, and another servant came with a silver box full of cocaine. He held a tiny spoon under her right nostril, and she sniffed. Chloe waved him off as she focused on the duchess's face. Her defeated and very dumb husband sat next to her. He had asked for the peacock's head and was making it talk to his uncle with a cartoon voice.

"Which news?" Chloe did not like to admit that she knew very little news outside of the news Willem allowed her to know: crypto prices, Loots stock, Rick & Morty memes, the LootsSocial feeds.

"We purchased the LootsTruth package," the duchess said. That specialized tier provided the duchess and her husband a dedicated PR agent to supply them with a PowerPoint deck each week containing social media and internet monitorings of certain keywords. (Chloe imagined: the duchess's name, her dumbass charities, the social conversation around re-establishing the monarchy.)

"Oh, sweetie," the duchess said disingenuously, "I thought you would know." Chloe cocked an eyebrow. "Hunter is getting remarried," she said.

"In Guantanamo Bay?" Chloe said skeptically. The duchess picked up her phone, scrolled through slides, and handed it to Chloe:

#Free Hunter: Democratic-Republicans Rally Behind Prison Reform

• Over 60,000 mentions in one week, the highest ever for the release of those imprisoned under Free America Act charges, see attached word cloud for sentiment score, trending in positive direction for wealthy Americans.

• Hunter Meadows touching Zoom engagement (and pregnancy reveal!) to socially conscious influencer Cassie Morton has >2 million views on YouTube.

• **RECOMMENDATION:** The duchess should call for his release from prison with time served, appeal to true love, family, children, etc. Do not mention the "American Dream" as that still has negative sentiment. See attached polling report on "How relevant Americans think the American Dream is?" and proposed social copy.

Chloe asked for another bump of cocaine as she turned this information over in her head. Who the fuck was Cassie Morton? Chloe navigated to Instagram, available to the duchess, and typed her name in. The duchess tried to grab the phone, but Chloe twisted and held it out of her reach. Cassie Morton's bio read: "Activist, Founder @DisruptPrison, mama to be, media inquiries in the DMs." Chloe navigated to the first picture of Cassie spread-eagled with bodacious curves in a bikini in South Beach, her hand over a flat stomach. Chloe froze.

She looked just like Kim Kardashian. The same long hair, the huge tits, the gigantic manufactured ass, the same smirk, the same big sunglasses. The caption read:

The boo and I fell in love over the written word. Correspondence on weathered, yellow letterhead, bonding over past traumas, his broken heart from loving someone suffering from Borderline Personality Disorder, and in his own confinement: the trauma from 23 hours a day indoors, in a cell smaller than most people's closets. Our love blossomed from the heinous crimes perpetrated against him by the very people who were supposed to protect him. Did Hunter kill anybody? Did he sexually assault anybody? He committed crimes, but this punishment fits no crime. #FreeHunter and the rest of the individuals unfairly imprisoned without trial under the Free America Act. Prison doesn't work, treating people does. It's people like Chloe Thibodeaux who require our #mentalhealth resources.

Chloe read it again and again. No sexual assault? She remembered when Hunter had paid off a co-ed from his frat days. No murder? A whole section of Hunter's Wikipedia detailed a hit-and-run that left a 22-year-old mother dead on the side of the road, while Hunter was airlifted to his daddy's compound in Alpine, New Jersey. She clenched her fists, digging her fingernails into the palm of her hand. When she looked up, the entire royal family watched her uneasily.

"Oh baby," the duchess said, "I didn't know you suffered from such a disease." Her words were compassionate, but she had a gleeful expression on her face.

"I am over Hunter," Chloe said, "I filed for divorce, not him."

"I'm sure you are," the duchess said.

"I've been divorced five times," the sweating disgraced prince said.

"Who hasn't?" his brother said, clinking a glass of scotch against his.

"I'm with Willem," Chloe said. Where was he? For once, she could use his uncouth attitude. His shrill laugh. Though she was sure the duchess had waited until he'd left to share this bit of information with her.

"Of course, you are," the duchess nodded. She didn't believe Chloe. Hunter said that Chloe had borderline personality disorder so now she was an unreliable narrator of her own life. The fucking asshole. Maybe he wasn't as dumb as she thought he was, or maybe Cassie Morton was more savvy than she looked.

"Hunter is imprisoned because he was a slumlord. He invented fees to evict people who'd lived in his buildings for years. He bankrupted people. Put them on the street."

"Just the cost of doing business though," a duke said. Of course he would say that, dukes invented feudalism, why would they think any different? And why should she? It was something Chloe would have said just an hour ago.

"Excuse me," she said, and headed towards Willem's computer room. He was watching a middle-aged bikini-clad woman in a blow-up bathtub write the names of her followers on her forehead with a permanent marker while annihilating someone with a tank on another screen. So, this was the important message. When he saw her, he put his hand on her ass.

"I remember watching this Twitch queen and jerking off when I was only forty years-old," he said wistfully. "The dalliances of youth, *eheuheuheuheu*."

"Can I borrow your phone?" Chloe asked.

"Why?" Willem said, without looking at her. The girl started whispering soothing nonsense into a microphone.

"I want to post the picture of us from Disney onto social media," she said. He'd taken her on a "date" the other day where he dressed her in a gold, metallic bikini and shackled her to an animatronic slug from a movie she had never seen before.

Willem sighed loudly and farted at the same time. She continued: "Baby, I know marketing. You know everything else. Do you want me to be your First Lady or not? If you gave me my own socials, that'd be one thing..."

"Mark is on his island in a cell-free pod," Willem complained, his same excuse for weeks now as far as why he hadn't advocated for her reactivation. "Fine," he sighed. "One picture."

He pulled up his feed and posted the picture with the caption: #69 lol. He kissed her, leaving a bit of saliva on the side of her mouth. Then examined her. She was impatient, uncomfortable in the tight gown. She wanted another bump of cocaine.

"Let me show you something," he said. "Mariko," he called out. She appeared in the doorway. "Get a Pegasus ready to take us to the stadium."

"Certainly," she said and vanished.

"What about the royals?" Chloe said.

"Fuck 'em," Willem said. He held out his arm and she took it.

Thirty-Two

September 20, 2038 | Loots Town

Moore was proud of Sasha. She'd worked hard and long into the night, eliminating any need for him to create a diversion to get her out. Sasha stretched the day as long as possible. She'd asked for a full video team and set a rigorous 12-hour production schedule. She'd examined every square foot of Yurts Town and wrote pages of tweets, scripts, talking points, hyper focused on triple checking everything. LootsWeb was happy with her hyper-focused work—notifications popped up saying *You go girl!* and *Hustle!* as the sun sank and the workers filed out of the construction site. She'd worked until there was literally nothing else left.

Moore checked his watch. It was almost go-time. He collected Sasha, whose nerves were finally beginning to show. He wished he could reassure her that he was on her side, but he couldn't risk it. The wind howled through the valley.

"Emmanuel," he said to the very fat and exhausted photographer. "Mariko wants you in Yurt 69." Emmanuel perked up at that. The sex bot yurt club. "For a job well done," Moore said and winked.

"Yes, sir," he said, licking his lips and rubbing his hands together.

"Where is he going?" Sasha asked over the wind.

"Oh, just some b-roll," he said. "He'll get a Pegasus back later. Come on," he motioned to her. He got in the driver's seat.

"You can actually *drive* these things?" she asked.

"Sure, it's a security thing," he lied. He hoped her mission was an American military operation. Moore would love to murder many people in Loots Town. It took some engineering to turn off the self-driving mod, a trick he'd learned on the streets of São Paulo when Willem Loots had used it as his bloody testing ground for the original self-driving tech. *Carros da morte*, everyone called them. The cars of death.

When Sasha was secure in the back seat, he opened the glove box and produced a knife.

"What is that?" Sasha asked in alarm.

"We don't have much time," he said. He dug the knife into his arm. The blood ran down his arm until he felt the smooth black chip. He fished it out, crushed it between his fingers, and threw it out the window. He accelerated towards the stadium south of town.

"I heard your conversation," he said. In the rearview mirror, he saw her clutch the armrest. "I'm helping you get out."

"Why?" she asked, suspiciously.

"I need to get out too."

"Aren't you spying on me?"

"Yes," he nodded vigorously. "It's why I need to get out. This place is evil."

"You're not the one imprisoned though," she said.

"Yes, I am. It's much, much worse for us. You will see." He gave her a sad smile as he sped towards the eSports Stadium.

The mine.

Thirty-Three

September 20, 2038 | Loots eSports Stadium

Chloe and Willem went through a series of checkpoints to get to the sphere rising from the desert. Each guard straightened up and saluted Willem as they passed through. Outside the entrance to the dome, they got out. She blinked in the floodlights. The place was crawling, not with guards, but with soldiers in desert camouflage with gigantic L's on their back, like a squadron full of losers. When they saw Willem, the soldiers immediately formed a line creating a pathway for them. A man with a Russian accent met them at a gigantic set of double-doors.

"Commander Loots," he said. "Your arrival is unexpected but greatly appreciated."

"I wanted to give my bride-to-be a tour," Willem said. The guard smiled at Chloe. He was missing teeth. The doors lurched open with a loud screech of metal. He led them in, barking orders.

Inside, stadium seating surrounded an enormous indoor military camp. In one area, shirtless men lifted weights. In another, a sergeant drilled a group of trainees, smacking them across the face if they faltered. At another station, men and women assembled and disassembled machine guns while a lieutenant weaved through them, observing with a stopwatch in his hand. The Russians were in charge and she could tell most of the trainees were Americans. Skinny and disheveled, straight from the streets of inner cities. The people who weren't training were sitting under makeshift shelters that Chloe supposed were residences. They played cards, drank whiskey, and smoked cigarettes. The room was warm.

"Underneath is a LootCoin mining facility," Willem explained. Chloe nodded as if that made sense to her.

They passed a room where a teenager sat strapped to a chair, unconscious and bleeding. A soldier noticed her looking and slammed the door. The man, whom Willem referred to simply as the Chechen, led them to a luxury suite that served as a dais looking over the whole operation.

This is what UDDR was really for. Willem had built an army.

"They're working around the clock on the expedited timeline," the Chechen said. "We will be ready by 0600."

"Ready for what?" she asked.

"Loots Nation," Willem grinned. *Shit*, Chloe thought. He was really going to do it. He was going to kill the Communist President. Tomorrow.

"Wow," she breathed. She was impressed. The man had vision.

"I knew you would like it." He kissed her for a long time, his tongue jabbing into her mouth and licking her teeth. She kissed him back.

All her resentment about Hunter's new marriage drained away. If this worked out, she would be able to kill him. For the first time in a long time, she was kind of turned on.

He pulled away. "I'll tell you everything, but first. The show."

Thirty-Four

September 20, 2038 | Loots eSports Stadium

Jay had never been to the eSports stadium. The construction workers assigned to that project lived on site. He didn't even know anybody who worked on it. After lights out, he crept out of his bed and into the desert. He had squirreled away extra water and protein bars all day to prepare for the four-mile trek across the desert. He was surprised he'd made it this far. Maybe Kenny had held out. There were no guards. There was nowhere to go, only miles and miles of empty desert all the way to the perimeter wall. It was like a gulag in that way, why guard people when there was no escape?

Jay had grown stronger from his months of hard labor. The hike wasn't hard. He only hoped Sasha had found a way to get out. What did surprise him was the level of security outside the sphere. The darkness provided cover as he crept past checkpoints along the highway illuminated by flood lights. The stadium was huge, bigger than a professional football stadium. He scaled the perimeter of the dome. Crates and construction equipment provided a decent amount of cover. At the north end, he heard someone say his name. He found Felix, Sasha, and her incredibly attractive servant, Moore. They looked nervous.

"This was too easy," Moore said to Felix. "There are usually patrols. Loots doesn't want people coming this close to the mine."

"The mine?" Jay asked.

"This is not a stadium," Moore said. "It's a camp. Haven't you wondered where the power in Loots Town comes from?"

"Solar panels?" Sasha asked. Moore snorted.

"That stadium is a work camp and distribution center. Gasoline, supplies, coal, and people come in through here. It's where I came in. From Brazil." Jay noticed smokestacks rising from the ground, letting out a noxious-looking gas.

Loots was running a slave camp. It truly was a gulag.

"I have pictures," Felix said. "It should be enough to get Loots arrested under the Free America Act. There is a breach in the wall near the mountains where a team is waiting."

"Thank God," Sasha breathed. "I am done being an activist."

"I'm telling you," Moore explained. "This was too easy."

An alarm screeched as they were lit up by drones. A group of soldiers materialized from behind the cover that Jay had been so thankful for earlier.

"Hands up, asshats," someone said in a Russian accent. The perimeter tightened around them. Jay shielded his eyes and then put his hands in the air. A drone whizzed down and examined the four of them.

"I knew it was the fucking Russians," Felix said.

"Lower your weapons," a familiar voice said. Jay's stomach clenched. His eyes adjusted and Lupe approached, in her trademark Dior suit and perfectly blown out hair.

"Hi Jay," she said with a smile. The soldiers began patting them down and tightening plastic restraints around their wrists. They pushed Jay roughly towards the door.

"You bitch," Jay said. "You treasonous bitch." Someone opened a door from the inside, and the soldiers led them inside single file.

"Sexist!" Lupe admonished. "Plus, I wouldn't cry treason from the guy who spent two months working for Willem Loots. What would the President say? He's been so sad since you've been gone. He called your dad a cocksucker. It's on all the news outlets. Our homophobic President. Polling isn't looking good," she tutted.

"What will he say when he finds out about you?" Jay growled.

"He won't," Felix said in a resigned tone. "He will be dead by tomorrow." Jay whirled around, before a soldier pushed him again.

"Face forward," he said.

"This was your plan?" Jay asked.

"I tried to stop it," Felix said.

"Such a shame," Lupe said. "Willem was going to make you deputy director of the CIA."

The soldiers pushed them through a shanty town set up in the stadium. Workers kept their eyes down. Jay saw doors made of shower curtains swish closed as they were marched in. Children carried buckets of rocks to a line of carts running underground. Sasha was mysteriously silent.

"Sasha, are you okay?" he called, not knowing where to look. Suddenly, they were in a clearing in the middle of the stadium. Hundreds of voices jeered them as they were marched by. Someone threw a bottle that smashed the ground right in front of him.

"Hello White House scum," a voice boomed. A giggle screeched through the speakers. "Trying to kill me?" Jay looked up and Willem Loots stood on a raised platform. Chloe Thibodeaux had her arm draped around him.

Thirty-Five

September 20, 2038 | Loots eSports Stadium

As they entered the stadium, a group of soldiers guided Sasha and Moore away from Jay and Felix. Overwhelmed, unable to get her bearings, she heard the sounds of stomping feet, cheers and boos, before being led underground through a series of winding hallways. She tried to keep track of the turns but couldn't.

"I didn't know," Sasha said in vain, thinking of Maya. Thinking of what they'd do to her. She would sell out anyone.

"It's no use," Moore told her. The soldiers kept a firm grip on them. Sasha recognized Lupe Fox, the senator turned chief of staff known for being a progressive Instagram star. Sasha had found comfort in her upbeat, but still revolutionary, calls at radical self-care when she was at her lowest points under Kim. If she was here, something big was happening. It smelled like smelting nickel. The temperature rose greatly. She coughed.

"It is ventilated out, but not very fast so the U.S. satellites do not see," Moore said quietly from in front of her. "Many friends of mine have died from gas sickness," he said. "Or nearly died, they are carted away and they do not come back."

"What are they for?" Sasha asked.

"Powering Loots Town and powering Loots Coin," he said.

"A Loots patented energy extraction technique. They don't tell us what exactly. Something like coal, but worse," he said. A rumble ran through the ground, like moaning from the earth.

"Shut up," a soldier said and hit Moore across the face. Sasha cried out. The soldiers then opened a door and shoved them into a windowless room.

"Are you okay?" she said, as the door shut and a lock clicked behind them.

"If you get out, you need to tell them," Moore said, blood running from his nose. "Fracking powers Loots Town. They found a lithium pocket too. Everything in the mine serves many purposes."

"How does the government not know?" she asked.

"Nobody in Loots Slum gets out," he said.

"You did," she said. "You live in the cabanas with me."

He smiled with cold eyes. "It took me a year to get outside, and I am monitored, same as you." He held up his bloody arm, he had torn a piece of his shirt to form a makeshift bandage. "At least you get drugs. I just got my life taken away," he said.

"What's your real name?" she asked.

"Márcio," he said.

"Márcio," she replied. The door burst open and a group of soldiers in helmets rushed in and swarmed them.

"Save your niece. Tell my wife I'm sorry," he said and then one of the soldiers shot him in the face. Márcio's blood splattered across her pencil skirt.

"Fuck," she cried out. "Fuck. Fuck. Fuck." She couldn't stop saying fuck.

"Hey," a soldier said, kneeling in front of her. She squirmed away from him. She was going to die in this shithole. Maya was going to die. She did this all for Maya and she was going to get her killed. "It's okay." She hyperventilated, trying to get out of the soldier's grip. The soldier in front of her unclicked his helmet.

It was Dima.

Sasha slid to the floor, limp in the soldier's arms.

Thirty-Six

September 20, 2038 | Loots eSports Stadium

"We found them," Lupe Fox said triumphantly as she led two men into the center of the chanting army. Willem held Chloe's hand as they walked to the center of the stadium. Chloe blinked at Lupe. Was the President's chief of staff really in Loots Tower doing Willem's *bidding* right now? Chloe remembered a statement Lupe had made about how Chloe's flight to Russia reopened traumatic wounds inflicted by the second Civil War. In fact, Lupe had conducted many interviews about Hunter Meadows and his bitch wife. Even before the Communist President. She had said he was a slumlord. The 1%. Lupe continued: "Sasha Ivanov too. She's being taken to a cell."

"Thank you, Lupe," Willem said. Chloe squinted at the two. One she vaguely recognized as an advisor to President Lopez. He glared up at them. The other tried to block his face from the projectiles flung by the soldiers. "This is unexpected but great, actually. An audience for my speech. It's good practice, my coach says, to 'vibe' in front of people before a big public speaking event and my life is about to get *very* public." Something strange came over Willem then, his voice became logical and toneless, his eyes drained of their quirk until they looked like two computers gazing over the stadium.

"We planned for a socialist President, an obnoxious President, one that levied taxes or gave handouts to the lazy masses. It wasn't a stretch to think *that* would happen, what with the destruction of Miami, the endless pandemics, the great western wildfires of 2034, and of course the Civil War," Willem said. The soldiers, his audience, laughed and hurled more projectiles.

The White House aide laughed.

"Shut up, Jay," Lupe said.

"Human suffering is funny to you?" Willem asked in his detached toneless voice that Chloe supposed was his "public speaking" voice. Willem nodded to a soldier who took off her helmet. Mariko kicked him in the side. He keeled over in pain. "Please no interruptions!" He smiled then, broadly, then continued: "Then they killed Kim Kardashian," he said. "Murdered her! One of us! We planned for some puny infrastructure bill or taxes we'd have to avoid but we didn't plan on actual killing, just for being rich. Some may say she created an environmental disaster but that wasn't her! That was the people who *worked* for her and if we're getting criminalized for our employees and put into Cuban gulags, I don't see how that's any different than the Nazis. It's time to de-Nazify America, and it starts with killing the Communist President!" The Russians pounded their feet on the ground.

"Loots Industries has always been about innovating, vision, the future, and now I'm going to innovate the United States of America by terraforming Nevada into the majestic, tropical paradise it once was thousands of years ago," he pressed a button and a jumbotron displayed a heavily CGIed clip of fat palm trees, enormous ferns blanketing the earth with canals meandering through bright foliage. A dinosaur casually fed on the carcass of a smaller dinosaur in a flat lowland next to the mountains. Chloe arched an eyebrow. She wasn't sure if this idea was actually possible, but her husband-to-be had surprised her before with doing the impossible. "This will no longer be a wasteland but a paradise!"

The crowd roared again.

"So beautiful, this is the kind of aggressive climate policy I advocated for at the beginning of my career," Lupe said with pride.

"We will turn the tides of climate change and populate this new world with beautiful, perfect babies!"

"Oh great, eugenics," Jay complained, and Mariko kicked him again.

"We're already working on terraforming Nevada with the same technology we will use on Mars to create Loots Nation, and soon Loots Galaxy! Tomorrow," he roared, "we will murder the President. Myself and a small, but formidable force of billionaires, will insert a new President to put this country on the right course. Me!"

"You're going to assassinate the President and just assume that it's all going to work out?" Jay asked.

"He started it by murdering *my* people," Willem said. "And yes, it's going to work out, because I have assurances from the highest levels of Congress that this will indeed come to pass," Willem said. He turned to face Jay. "Your presence here is indeed strange. At first, I thought you came to spy on us, but maybe you really came because you are lost. You should join me."

Jay spat on the ground. "Good luck getting Lopez in D.C."

"Oh, he's here, in Vegas," Willem said. "And he will *burn*."

This version of Willem was beginning to unsettle Chloe. He seemed less malleable. More prone to erratic violence. But here she was! Either his plan was brilliant or idiotic, and until she knew the exact answer, or had another option, she had to stick with him.

"Babe, what should we do with this leftist scum?" Willem asked. The crowd was raging now, close to boiling over. Something tugged at Chloe. She wanted to stay on Willem's side, but she did not want to be directly responsible for this man's death. He was just a peon. She vaguely remembered that the President was his childhood friend. He didn't deserve to die. She glanced at Lupe. The woman might be on their side now, but *she* was the one who got Chloe here. If it wasn't for her, she would be living in a mansion in Marin County. She *did* deserve something.

"Two White House officials spying on Loots Town? It's an

act of war," she said. Lupe clicked her eyes onto Chloe in alarm. "These hypocrites spying after all that talk about the NSA, the martyr Julian Assange, Hunter Meadows. They're full of shit. They just want your stuff. Just like they want everyone's stuff. More than enough reason to gather a resistance and march on Washington."

"Holy shit," Willem said in his normal voice. "That's a great idea." He nodded to the Chechen, who handed him a flamethrower.

"What?" Lupe said, outraged. "No. No. Bad plan."

"Great plan!" Willem said with pride. He put his hand on Chloe's ass and squeezed it. A few soldiers grabbed Lupe and forced her to her knees.

"You said I would be made a Supreme Court justice," Lupe said weakly.

"Gotta take one for the team for our climate-positive future!" Willem said and held up the flamethrower.

"Wait," Chloe said. "They're useful hostages."

"Of course," Willem said, lowering the weapon. "What about the CIA guy?"

Chloe shrugged. She had no love for the CIA. As far as she was concerned, he could burn. The presence of the flamethrower meant someone had to. Mariko brought him forward and threw him onto the ground. To his credit, he didn't beg for his life.

Before Mariko could get out of the way, Willem pulled down on the trigger of his flamethrower. The man erupted in flames but so did Mariko. She screamed as the flesh peeled from an electric arm. When he stopped, the entire side of her face melted, revealing human parts dripping and scalded alongside charred metal and computer parts.

"Oops," Willem said. The CIA agent fell to the ground. Soldiers used a fire extinguisher to put out Mariko but not before she was a mutated, cowering cyborg. "Oh well. You were reaching the end of your shelf life anyway. You are an underground person now. A minion! Now take these people to prison and prepare for the Battle of Las Vegas!" Willem bellowed.

Mariko looked at him, bleeding from some places, her

remaining eye bobbing precariously, and for a moment Chloe thought Mariko would leap at him and bite him, but instead she took the two prisoners by their collars and dragged them from the arena. The crowd had totally lost it. Men chugged vodka. Others screamed. Dogs had come and were snapping at the burning corpse of the CIA agent.

"Glad that's done," Willem said, "Let's go home. I want to have sex before I'm President. *Eheuheuheuheu*."

Thirty-Seven

September 20, 2038 | Loots eSports Stadium

Mariko's head throbbed, but that wasn't because her body was slowly melting. It had been like that for a long time. Ten years ago, she was a model living in Tokyo. She'd done a few photo shoots, but mostly she just handed out flyers for a fashion shop in Harajuku.

A rich American stopped in front of the shop and licked his lips.

"Do you want a job?" he asked.

Some quick money off a rich Gaijin with a Japanese fetish? Why not?

At first, the job was easy. The rich American turned out to be the *richest* American, Willem Loots. All she had to do was stand next to Willem and make him look important in front of all of his investors and employees. She enjoyed the private plane rides, running her hands along the soft fabric of designer gowns, stitched to her body so she shined in the darkness like a glittering diamond. It didn't matter that, really, she was just a possession, like all of his others, meant to signal to those around him just how much he'd *made it*.

Then Willem started bringing up Cort-X.

It was one of Loots's menagerie of companies. One of many

that already existed, which he had purchased and then acted as though it was his invention. Cort-X was doing cutting edge research, Willem told Mariko. They'd put digital brain implants into test animals that had increased their cognitive ability tenfold, he claimed.

It could turn normal people into superheroes, he insisted.

He started subtly implying that Mariko should consider the procedure. When she didn't respond, he began to suggest it with less subtlety. He offered her the surgery, which he promised was completely safe, free of charge. Then he offered to pay her extra for it. An exorbitant amount. She had a poor family back in San'ya.

She agreed to the surgery.

She found out later that the test results with the chimps had all been fudged before release to the investors. They had excised results that they had deemed "outliers." Outliers like when a chimp died from a massive brain hemorrhage during the procedure.

Mariko's health problems began shortly after the surgery. Her body was in pain constantly, as it tried to reject the unnatural implants. She became even more dependent on Loots for treatments for the ailments that he had caused her. She looked like the same, beautiful woman in the mirror but on the inside, she *hurt*, like nothing she had ever experienced before. She became addicted to painkillers, on a constant regiment of antibiotics for the never-ending infections.

Aside from the health complications, the implants actually worked. Her cybernetic eye displayed a constantly running feed of social media and news and sent a digital live feed of everything she saw. A subdermal implant in her ear connected her permanently to her boss.

Her pain didn't matter. All that mattered to Willem Loots was his having a "real-life Ghost in the Shell."

She bore it all. She was working her way up the ranks. One day she would be more powerful than he was, and on that day, she would kill him. All of this would be hers.

Then he lit her on fire.

Thirty-Eight

September 20, 2038 | LootsPrison

"Just let us shoot her!" Sasha heard one of the soldiers say. She couldn't stop looking at Moore's body. She had never seen so much blood before. In the movies, it didn't look so thick, that there was so much of it, full of chunks of tissue and flesh. He had a wife and children, and now he was a puddle. A group of soldiers dragged Moore off, leaving a smear of blood in his wake.

"Are you sure we can't shoot her, boss?" another soldier said in Russian. He was the only soldier left in the room besides Dima.

"No!" Dima exclaimed, and then to the soldier in Russian: "Loots wants her alive."

"Boss, huh?" Sasha said. "I thought you were a carpenter."

Dima was quiet for a moment and then said in a low voice, "The drugs you were talking about. How do you–"

The Russian soldier interrupted him and said: "You are going to take this from inferior, fat woman?" He crossed his arms, clearly bored. Dima pulled Sasha to her feet roughly.

"These fucking things," the Russian took off the helmet and revealed a huge, sweaty beard and pock-marked face. Sasha recognized him as the Chechen from LootsGun Instagram videos. He looked Sasha up and down. "Not very pretty, but I will rape her before we kill her, no?" he said. Sasha felt Dima stiffen.

"Shut up, dickless shitbrain," Sasha said to the soldier in Russian.

"Russian, too! Now, I really want to rape her."

"I don't like that talk," a female voice said, wavering, as if through an old radio. The half-melted Mariko. "Sexual assault is not a joking matter, Ramzan. Believe women."

Ramzan scoffed. "Who's joking?"

"The Chechen wants you for the briefing," Mariko said. It was hard for Sasha to look at her, and the *smell*, a short-circuiting piece of human flesh.

She was still smoking.

Ramzan took a long look at Sasha, made an obscene gesture and then as he was leaving, Mariko clotheslined him with her electronic arm. He fell to the ground, coughing. She then kicked him in the head. He fell limp. Even Dima was surprised by this. He turned to Mariko. It was clear he reported to her. Waiting.

"Undo her restraints," Mariko said.

"But Willem," Dima said. Fear flashed across his eyes.

"Willem Loots isn't in charge anymore," Mariko said.

Dima did as he was told.

THIRTY-NINE

September 21, 2038 | LootsPrison

Jay sat on the hard bench. Lupe sat directly across from him with her head in her hands. Willem, as a joke, had planted a flatscreen in the cell tuned to CNNBC. A shot of double-chinned Jay with pit stains coordinating campaign efforts in 2036, and one of a coiffed Lupe touting nails that read "VOTE" permanently plastered half the screen.

The only thing Jay could think of was that he wished CNNBC had used a more flattering picture.

On the screen, the pundits blathered breathlessly about the President's illegal espionage at the hands of the most senior members of his administration. It was probably the most positive mentions of the Free America act (for its corporate espionage clauses) from pundits in history. An incendiary chyron blared:

BREAKING NEWS: *WHITE HOUSE SPYING ON SOVEREIGN LOOTS TOWN. WILLEM LOOTS EXPECTED TO SPEAK SOON.*

. . .

Gray-haired, august Jake Tapper led an unwieldy, free-wheeling back-and-forth with his panelists:

"I'm hearing President Lopez has refused to comment on the allegations."

"This is, sadly, typical for the guillotine regime, isn't it?"

"I'm just saying, targeting an environmentalist like Willem Loots really reveals the President's lack of prioritizing climate."

"Is Ashton Kutcher being spied on?"

Jay found it hard to breathe normally in the small cell. He had tweeted this before. *Studies show cable news lights up the fear centers of the brain.*

"You really backed the right horse, didn't you, Lupe?" Jay spat at his cellmate.

Lupe shook her hanging head. "You have no fucking clue. You and Pablo have always been clueless. I actually have ambition. I want to make this country better. You just want to kill rich people."

Guilty as charged. "The way I see it, if we'd acted on my plan to investigate Willem Loots, then you and I wouldn't be sitting in this cell." He waved at the flatscreen. "We wouldn't be framed for *all of this.*"

Lupe looked up from her hands, her face twisted in fury. "Framed? *Framed?!* You aren't being framed, Jay, you *were* here spying on Loots Town. *I'm* the one being fucking framed here. I'm the one who tried to play ball, with both sides, and look where it got me." She shook her head, a distant look in her eyes. "I actually had a plan. I had a plan that could work for everyone. People like you, and Pablo, and Willem Loots... you're really all the same. *Men*, with no patience. You need it all now, because how else are you going to piss all over it and make your mark." She shook her head with disgust. She really truly hated him. "People didn't see, they didn't see. The APP people, the toxic, unrealistic lefties, they hated me for playing the game. For working the system for *what they wanted*. Meanwhile, everyone else hated me for being close to *you people*."

"Oh, boo-hoo," Jay responded, dismissively. "The poor

Senator in the Dior pantsuit was disliked by some people online. That must have been so hard for you."

"Laugh it up, Jay. I spent twenty fucking years in D.C. doing everything right. Waiting for the right moment to make a run for the White House. Then your buddy, on a whim, runs for the presidency. Because the APP didn't have anyone else to run, because he was a community organizer with B+ looks who could actually talk on TV. And," she laughed, "because he was a *man*." She laughed again, long and hard. "It was *my* turn."

"That's not democracy. That's the whole point of what I'm trying to do. It's not just each side politely taking turns at being President while pretending on television it's all about *democracy*."

"That works better," she grumbled.

"Oh yeah, it really worked out when Miami was destroyed because Senators couldn't decide which contractor to award the FEMA contract to."

"It didn't start a war," she said.

"We ended the Russian forever war. Does *anyone* remember that?" Jay's comms brain lit up. They really needed to amp up messaging about that.

"I'm not talking about that. You started a war that actually *mattered* on U.S. soil. You started a war with the rich. That's not a war we can win, Jay. If every so-called communist revolutionary shrieking about Molotov cocktails on Twitter took to the streets, it would take about fifteen minutes and a dozen drones to take care of it if things really got out of hand." She wiped her hands together. "But the rich are the ones who actually run this country. You know that, Jay, I've heard you say it a thousand times. What doesn't make sense is why, if you believe that, you thought they'd just lay down and take it. That they wouldn't fight back. But, still, you pushed the President into an unwinnable war with an infinitely powerful enemy, and why? Because you've got daddy issues." She mock cried, wiping fake tears from her eyes. "'Oh, Daddy wasn't nice to me! He moved away. Poor me!'" She snapped her head toward him with a steely glare. "Grow the fuck up, Jay."

Jay was furious. "You thought *that guy*." A video clip on CNNBC showed Willem Loots humping a rocket. "Was going to make you a Supreme Court justice?"

Before she could respond, a pair of Loots Military in reflective helmets brandishing assault rifles entered the cell. One of the guards retrieved a small electronic device and used it to work on a nearby wall panel.

Lupe lowered her voice, "They're the only ones with power. On the Supreme Court, I could really do some long-lasting good."

"See, I actually believe you believe that! That's your problem. You've got D.C. brain. If Willem Loots does an insurrection —an actual insurrection, by the way, not a bunch of rednecks vaping in a statehouse—there's not going to *be* a fucking Supreme Court anymore. That's what you don't understand about rich people. Sure, maybe I learned it from my dad, but I'm glad I got the lesson. They don't give a fuck about you, or anyone other than themselves. The power they offer you is fake. The rich will always chew you up and spit you out as soon as you're an inconvenience."

One of the guards approached the cell. "He's right," she said, eying him.

The other guard finished with the wall panel. "Surveillance is disabled. We've got a few minutes. It's now or never."

The guards slid their reflective visors back into their helmets. It was Sasha and a man Jay recognized as a chief yurts architect who he now noticed bore a striking resemblance to Sasha. Sasha nodded toward a door at the end of the hallway.

The door opened and, with some difficulty, the severely burned, semi-metallic, and partially melted Mariko hobbled in. She produced a keycard which she held up to a reader mounted on the wall. The cell door slid open.

Sasha turned to Jay. "Let's move. We've got to save the President. We can't let that incel fucker be President."

Jay stood and was surprised to find himself hugging her. "I'm glad you're okay," she whispered.

She tensed for a moment then hugged him back. "You too."

"We have ten seconds," Mariko said. Jay and Sasha released each other and began to file out of the cell. Dima followed. Before Lupe could exit, Mariko barred her way with the metal arm.

"You," she said, "Cannot be trusted." As she closed the doors behind them, Jay heard Lupe screaming "Wait! Take me with you! I can be useful! I know things! Don't leave me here!!!"

Then the door clicked shut.

For a malfunctioning android, Mariko was fast.

"Come *on*," Dima said as Jay and Sasha struggled to keep up.

"I'm sorry, am I going too *slow* for you?" Sasha replied. "I don't have much experience breaking out of prison that you, my beloved brother, put me in at the orders of an insane man."

"Really? Now? We're doing this now?" Dima replied.

"What is the proper etiquette for this situation then?"

"Siblings," Jay muttered.

The group turned a corner and almost barreled into Chewbacca—the Loots tunnels must share space with Real Tatooine—smoking a cigarette. He cursed at them and gave the finger as they passed by. Mariko waved her hand in front of a heavy door to reveal a train car.

"This is as far as I can go, I can only keep my feed scrambled for so long," she said. "I'll keep Willem in the dark as long as possible but be careful. He will find out soon." One eye blinked while the other lolled to the side in its bed of guts and circuitry. Sasha felt like she ought to hug her savior, but she didn't know if hugs would hurt Mariko.

Before she could make any move, Mariko's head exploded, revealing the toothless Chechen grinning as the train doors closed. Bullets pinged off the train as it moved.

Forty

September 21, 2038 | Loots Town Outskirts

Sasha spat out a piece of skull and wiped blood off her face, she stared at the gelatinous mass of metal and organs covering her hands and torso. The second time someone was brutally murdered in front of her in the last hour.

"Holy shit," Jay repeated over and over again after the train doors closed and the carriage began to move. "Her head blew up. Did Willem blow her head up? Do we have one of those?" Jay asked Dima nervously.

"Did you get brain surgery, moron?" Dima asked. He took his helmet off and pulled at the collar, sweating profusely, before sitting on the metal bench lining one side of the car. The car was packed with cargo crates.

"I don't know," Jay said, "Would we know? Fuck. Shit. God damnit."

"You would know," Sasha said, not knowing if that was true at all. She spit burnt crisps of Mariko's hair onto the ground. Her thoughts had unspooled to a single, terrifying thread: she needed to void the detritus of Mariko from her person.

"You need a shower," Dima said, handing her a handkerchief to wipe the blood from her face. "You don't want to be covered in blood when we see the Chechens. It would excite them too much. Just keep the fatigues on until I can get you to the latrines."

"Oh good," Jay said, "A military camp."

A vague memory tugged at her consciousness. "I sent Matt footage of Loots Slum," she said. "Hopefully, he released it."

"You did *what*?" Dima said. "What did I tell you? You can't *trust* that guy."

"It's a big, breaking story," she said, feeling stupid now. In only the way an older brother can make a sister feel.

"You really don't know him at all." The ground rumbled all around them as a rocket launched from the surface. "We need to go faster," Dima said.

Above ground, the bivouacs rose from the desert floor like neat lines of slugs fanned out from common areas with desert camouflage canopies where men readied ammunition, chowed on MREs, and played Xbox. The signage around the camp indicated it was a weekend long paintball "mission" for tourists to Yurts Town.

A paintball mission with an Iskander-M missile system mounted onto a carrier vehicle. Like, don't worry guys, it just shoots enormous paintballs.

It took all Dima's effort to keep going. All he could think of was returning to the barracks for another fix, an IV ostensibly full of "multivitamins" but was actually morphine. No wonder he felt so calm and sharp. He was on just enough to feel like he could do anything, which he assumed was the point. A complacent and nice little soldier thinking he was finally coming into his own sober self.

Willem Loots was a motherfucker.

He was due for another half-hour at the IV, and he felt it. His hands shook, he had to remind himself to breathe in big, gasping mouthfuls. His hands and feet tingled. This was the best part of it, the calm before the real withdrawal. At this point, it was mostly psychological. His mission was to get Sasha and her friend to safety but all he could think about was the IV. How could he get to the IV? One last fix for one last mission. A nonstop thought loop convincing himself to just hook himself up to the IV.

No. He couldn't. He had to stop. He was a mercenary deadbeat dad insurrectionist who had just arrested his own sister. If that wasn't rock bottom, he didn't know what was.

After he settled Sasha and Jay into a latrine tent with clean clothes, he weaved through the crowd of hyped up and bored soldiers (a bad combo) to his bunk. A plastic bag of suboxone was where Mariko said it would be. Starting tomorrow, this would be his life. A dull, plodding shitstain of a fix that would rule the rest of his life. He'd heard in an NA meeting on another failed sobriety journey that heroin changed neural pathways in the brain. Maybe he was going to feel this *need* forever.

When Dima left Las Vegas, he thought he was doing Maya a great service. He could only muster fatherhood in bursts. The project of his existence was a lost cause. At least he could make up for it by burying Willem Loots first.

Sasha was anxious at her lack of response to Mariko's death. She showered the blood off easily, combing bits of skull and microchip out of her hair without thinking that it once belonged to a (somewhat) whole person. In her fatigues and cap, she looked nothing like the Loots Town media darling. Her face was growing old, she discovered. Tired.

When she walked out, Jay stood with big aviator sunglasses and a baseball hat. "Stand in the back," Dima told them. Sasha examined a beefy guy with a gnarly face scar in slightly more professional looking military garb.

"Who is the guy in charge?" she asked.

"Lieutenant Steve," Dima said. "He fought in Ukraine and is a prolific poster on 8kun. Most of these guys are, besides the Chechens. They're the only ones you really have to worry about." Dima said.

"Ivanov!" Lieutenant Steve barked. Dima rushed to the front of the makeshift briefing. Soldiers sat on benches facing a projector screen. Dima stood next to another soldier behind the man who must be their superior. "Alright fuckers, we have new intel."

He pressed a button and a video played. Matt appeared on the screen with a microphone in his studio back in Vegas.

"Breaking news from your favorite anti-establishment podcast," he said, happily. "News that will shock you to your core, about a plot unfolding just outside my very own Las Vegas, Nevada." Sasha sighed in relief. He got the video. He was going to expose it and they could be done with this exercise in political intrigue. "I sat down with the one, the only, your favorite internet shit poster, Willem Loots." The screen flickered to Willem, sitting in a chair with his hair slicked back. Sasha froze.

"This is your first public interview in over five years, Mr. Loots," Matt said with a smug expression.

"What can I say? I believe in freedom of speech. Liberal cancel culture and our current political environment discourages that. Plus, I'm a very... concise man. I don't like talking at length. I use that brain space for innovation."

"Well, then what brings you here today?" Matt said. He was practically salivating.

"I felt the American people needed to see this," he said. "That's why I reached out to you. I wanted *the people* to know. I didn't want this suppressed by the powers that be. I thought these people were my friends, and they betrayed me. They betrayed the entire peaceful project of Loots Town. You will see that Pablo Lopez's plan is to become a dictator. Literally Hitler, except instead of Jews, it is our nation's brightest minds."

"With that, let's roll the tape," Matt said, and the screen faded into a grainy video.

Sasha sat in a pantsuit with perfectly coiffed hair. She remembered the outfit, one nixed by Moore before a CNNBC appearance. The background was not her cabana; however, but a dark industrial background, like some kind of underground lair.

Jay sat next to her in a suit and tie. Lupe wore her big glasses and trademark pantsuit with a grave expression on her face.

"We are in Loots Town on order of the President to infiltrate this independent innovation zone," Jay said. Sasha nodded at him thoughtfully. She remembered practicing that nod in front of the mirror before an NPR appearance.

"While we were only supposed to spy, what we found was astonishing. The wealthy, happy and flourishing, in peace," Lupe said.

"This cannot stand. Kim Kardashian was not enough," Sasha said.

"There is only one way to solve this problem," Jay said. "Kill the rich. Kill them all and take back this country."

"Wow, really serious stuff. Now, Willem, tell us a little more about life in Loots Town—" the lieutenant cut the footage. The troops murmured. A Chechen said, "I would fuck the fat one."

"Boys," he said. "The day we've been training for has come. We need to secure the streets from extremist leftist agitators." Dima caught Sasha's eye with a look that said see what I told you.

The men all cheered.

Jay had to admit that the video was good. He wanted to believe that Loots was bad at everything, that all his products were as broken as his cars, but Jay had to admit that the guy could make a deepfake. He itched for a phone. This video had to be everywhere. Sergeants handed out stills of the video to all the soldiers and said Loots wanted them, dead or alive. Sasha took Jay's arm and headed towards the back of the tent, facing away from the soldiers preparing for battle.

"There are cameras everywhere in Loots Town," Sasha told Jay, "He had a lot of footage of us to create the video with."

"Now we're embedded with the very men who want to kill us," Jay said.

"What's that?" Sasha asked. Jay looked over to where she

pointed. A gigantic green truck held up two rockets pointed in the direction of Las Vegas. A few operators checked equipment against a manual. Another one watched a YouTube video on his phone, frowning. He looked at the enormous launcher and back at the video, then fiddled with the truck's insides and cursed.

"Uh," Jay said. "That's a rocket launcher."

"Why does he need a rocket launcher?" Sasha asked.

Jay thought. "That crazy asshole is going to blow him up. Lopez is at an event tonight at the University of Nevada, Las Vegas. He's going to fucking *bomb* it."

Dima approached them. "We need to go."

"No way," Jay said. "We can call in a bomb threat no problem. Just drop us off in Pahrump where there is cell service."

"Yeah, there is no cell service," Dima replied. "Loots's satellites killed the cell service. We're in a dead zone. It's part of the plan."

"They're going to recognize us and murder us."

"Your disguises work," Dima said quietly. "Sasha, you are professionally made up in that video and you look like shit right now, no offense. Jay," Dima paused. "They're all racist. They wouldn't pick you out of a crowd even if you had no disguise. Now please, shut the fuck up and blend."

For the first time in his life, Jay thanked Daddy Racism.

Forty-One

September 21, 2038 | Loots Town Outskirts

The plan, Dima told them as they entered the back of a Humvee, was to secure the university, Harry Reid International Airport, and the South Strip. Three tactical groups were loaded into convoys of Humvees and Bradley Fighting Vehicles to secure the area against the "leftist agitators" (i.e., anyone wary about an armed insurrection). Dima was heading up the university group and could get Jay and Sasha to UNLV where Jay could rescue the President.

"Just waltz in and rescue the President, surrounded by the Secret Service, with my face on every television in the country," Jay said.

"It's a bad plan," Dima admitted, "but it's our only one. I'm going to try to get as many people away from campus as possible. Sasha, I advise you to do the same. Loots has air support."

Dima stood and yelled: "Okay Bravo Team. The mission is to surround and secure the area. No civilian casualties. We're here to protect people, not attack." Dima repeated the instructions in Russian to the Chechens who cheered. Dima whistled and the vehicle began to rumble down the valley towards Las Vegas.

It was an hour drive in a regular car without a retinue of troops. As they lumbered along, Sasha leaned over to Dima.

"Didn't realize you had any military skills," she said. She could be candid because their conversation was drowned out by the noise of the vehicle.

"Please don't use that tone with me," he said.

"What tone?"

"Like you haven't been in Loots Town doing Willem Loots's bidding too."

"Not war stuff," she said.

"Just war propaganda then," he said. "Much better."

"I came here looking for you."

"Why?" he asked, turning towards her.

"I told you, Maya—" she said.

"I know about Maya, and you could have found the insulin, especially with your new friend from the White House. Hell, I would've signed for the artificial pancreas and sent you on your way. You didn't have to take it this far. Why are you always doing this?"

"Because you always make it about you! You want us all to come save you!" Sasha exclaimed. "Since we were kids, you were the one with the big, flashy problems. The ones mom and dad were always hyper focused on. The one who needed help."

Dima's personality was bigger than life. A fruit fly she swatted at which never left her alone while it tried to get at the sweet moisture of her dripping eyeballs. When it wasn't heroin, it was his brain! He got expelled from school yet made incredible tapestries their mother would hang in her house. His photographic memory! The way he could go off and become a builder, a soldier, whatever he wanted, and even though most of the time he was a junkie, people saw him for what he could be as opposed to what he was. Even when she prospered in LA, her family could only see Dima. He was always the delight of their family during cookouts on Olga's houseboat on Pyramid Lake. Handsome man! Poetic man! Extraordinary man! He hurt people in these beautiful, all-consuming ways that worked them into a froth of intoxicated distraction, and then asked why they even cared about him. Even when she was on television, the whistle-blower of the century, her parents only thought of Dima. Was he okay? She remembered Dima's breakups and triumphs more vividly than her own because he made himself the center of people's lives. She tried to explain this to him over the roar of the military equipment. During her speech, one group raised a Nazi flag, was yelled at and hastily pulled it back down again. Another explosion from Loots Town rumbled the ground.

"You wanted me to follow you. For us all to," she continued. "That's all you've ever wanted. You are selfish. Even now, saving my life, it's not even about me, or about Maya, it's about you. So, don't act like you don't want the attention."

"I'm trying to be better," he said, quietly. He was crying a little bit. Even his tears were more beautiful than hers.

"God, shut the fuck up," she said. Another explosion rumbled, and even though she hated him, she took his hand and squeezed it. He squeezed back.

Jay watched them and couldn't help but think of Pablo, the closest thing he had to a brother. The siblings didn't speak again as the convoy gained speed on the trip down the mountain and the Strip came into view.

Forty-Two

September 21, 2038 | Las Vegas Strip

Sasha told Jay that malaise was normal for Las Vegas, but he found it astonishing that nobody gave the militia a second glance as they pulled up on Tropicana on the south side of the UNLV campus and started blocking traffic. Soldiers filed out and fanned out in groups, clutching machine guns. A group of cops watched them from the hood of their car eating Taco Bell.

"The President is in one of the ballrooms in the Thomas & Mack Center. VP is in Cox Pavilion," Dima told them. He handed them both earpieces. He tore off the Velcro Ls on their backs and took their helmets, giving them black baseball hats. "This is a private channel so we can all communicate. If there is any trouble—"

"We'll figure it out," Sasha said. "I can show you where to go." They jogged towards the towering parking lot surrounding the arena. He expected there to be security, but it looked like any other rodeo or basketball game on campus. Flaggers directed minivans to parking along the perimeter, ignoring the troops infiltrating the area. Students waved. Some encouraged them to *protect our President*, others yelled to *murder the fucker*.

The closer they got to the President, more barriers popped up, metal detectors, and additional guards. Since the video had just broken, the men were a logistical mess, talking on phones, asking for more backup. From the curses spewed, Jay gathered there wasn't any. Nobody seemed to know what to do.

They walked around the arena until Jay spotted what he was looking for. A side entrance guarded by a Secret Service guy that Jay fucked once. As he expected, the guy was engrossed with swiping through Grindr. He didn't look up as they approached.

"National Guard," Jay said, lowering his voice an octave. "We're here to provide extra protection per the January 6 Security Act. We need to inspect the arena for explosive devices following Willem Loots's statement," he said. The guy didn't even look up.

"J6, of course, go on," he waved them into the complex.

"Great operation you have here," Sasha told him as they entered the deserted concourse. She led them to the ballroom Dima indicated, the doors flanked by security officials. "Lupe Fox and Jay Betteta were spotted by Lied Library," the two blinked at her, as Jay faced the other direction. "Code red, motherfuckers! Go, go, go!" The two stiffened and sprinted off.

"I guess Code Red is a thing," Sasha said. "It's your turn now. I'll let you know if I spot incoming missiles." She tapped her right ear. Jay took a deep breath and pulled open the doors to the ballroom.

The room was big and empty with high-tops around with cold, unappealing appetizers. A small group of people were huddled around a screen. A CNNBC anchor was speaking on mute in front of the video of Sasha, Jay, and Lupe. The video dissolved into footage from cities across America that had broken into protests.

"Mr. President," a Secret Service agent that Jay didn't recognize said. "You need to get out of here. This could go either way. The people are turning on you and we don't have the resources to stop them."

"Don't I give you billions of dollars per year to protect me?" Pablo asked. "I'm not going anywhere."

"Air Force One is fueled up at Harry Reid," the goon said nervously.

"Pablo," Jay said. The group turned, puzzled at his appearance. Jay sighed and took off his sunglasses and hat. The Secret Service immediately drew their weapons. Pablo stared down his old friend.

"Permission to shoot, sir," the goon said.

"Permission denied," Pablo said.

"He's right, Pablo," Jay said. "You need to get out. Loots is planning to kill you. He's sending a drone. Now," Jay said.

"What?" The Secret Service agent went pale.

"I came to warn you," Jay said.

"Why should I believe you?" Pablo said. The Secret Service guys exchanged glances. It probably wasn't the time for this argument.

"So, uh, you're not going anywhere, Mr. President?" the goon asked. Pablo shook his head. The Secret Service nodded to each other and then ran for the exits. The group of advisors followed, leaving Jay and Pablo alone.

"Great operation you have here," Jay said. "Leaving you alone with a known agitator."

"Are you?" Pablo asked.

"What do you think?"

"I think you disappeared months ago."

"I had to prove to you that Willem Loots was a fucking villain. You were being sucked into the Beltway nonsense. The same nonsense you promised you wouldn't get sucked into. I had to make you see what he was doing so we could stop him and actually do some good instead of some pretend half measures motioning towards maybe doing gun control someday. You said we *wouldn't* be that way."

"You abandoned me! What was I supposed to do? I can't do this all alone," Pablo said. "You were supposed to keep me in check. To hold me accountable."

"You're constantly surrounded by people who can do that," Jay said.

"They want me to fail," Pablo said. "I disrupt their plans for future paychecks." Pablo looked down. "Plus, they aren't my brother."

Jay froze at that and thought back to Sasha and Dima's exchange on the ride down. Their brutal argument that ended in an embrace, a tacit understanding that they would protect each other. *That's what siblings do,* Jay thought. *They disappear, they piss you off, they let you down, they drive you crazy, and then they protect you for it.*

"What'd you find out?" Pablo asked. "Despite the obvious," he said as a news anchor melted down on live television over the hypocritical regime.

"He's plotting with fucking Jacky Cohn of all people to assassinate you and replace you as President," Jay said.

"That fucking cunt," Pablo complained. "How do you know all this?"

"He told me," Jay said. "Lupe too. By the way, she committed treason to become a Supreme Court justice."

"Goddamnit," Pablo said. "I fucking hate being President."

"And now, Willem Loots is set to address the nation," the gleeful anchor said. "In 3, 2, 1..."

"We gotta go," Jay said, but Pablo held up a hand, watching the screen.

Forty-Three

September 21, 2038 | Loots Town

When Willem told Chloe he was going on live TV to address the nation, she thought he was pulling some kind of James Bond villain taking over the airwaves thing. As it turned out, he simply had Loots Town PR representatives email their contacts at the various cable news channels and they all agreed to carry his planned address live.

Chloe scowled at the camera crew as they prepared the study to broadcast Willem to the world. Willem sat behind the desk as a makeup artist powdered his face so that he wouldn't look so old on camera. Chloe spent the preceding hour applying her own makeup. The help might be good enough for Willem, but she had her brand to think about here. They both knew that it would all come down to this appearance. This one was for all the marbles.

The makeup lady applied the finishing touches as Willem read his prepared remarks from the Notes app on his phone. Chloe stared deeply at him, sincerely uncertain about how this would end up. A team of Hollywood writers living in Loots Tower, headed by Aaron Sorkin, had written the speech for him. As written, it was stirring. But if Chloe was being honest with herself, she wasn't totally sure if Willem had the charisma to pull it off on-camera. He had managed somehow to pull off years of product unveilings and TED Talks, but this time was different. This time he wasn't flanked by flashy tech or trying to win over credulous investors who *wanted* to believe in him, he was trying to win over the famously fickle American public. Americans mostly loved the wealthy, so he had that in his favor. But also, on a gut level, they hated weirdos and nerds.

This could go either way.

Willem took his place in front of his desk, standing on a position marked with a taped "T" on the floor. Chloe took her position on the "T" mark at his side. "Stand up straight," she said as she pressed on his rounded upper back. He straightened up. "You're going to do great," she told him, trying to convince herself as much as him.

He looked at her with a smile. "Here goes nothing, *eheuheuheu*."

She smiled back, stifling an internal cringe. *He better not do that giggle on TV*, she thought. She hooked her arm in his and leaned against him, affecting her best "loving wife" body language. The aging rocker behind the camera counted down from five on his fingers, and then gave Willem a point. A red light on the camera popped on. Willem was live.

"Hello, my fellow Americans," he began. "I am Willem Loots, the leader of Loots Town sovereign innovation zone. I'm joined here by my beautiful wife, Chloe Thibodeaux-Loots." Were they married? Did they get married and she didn't realize it? No matter, Chloe smiled and nodded slightly to the camera before slipping her arm from Willem's and stepping out of frame, as was the pre-planned choreography. She was meant to be there only for a moment to remind the Americans watching that Willem was not only wildly wealthy, but he had a hot wife.

Outside of camera view, she no longer had to plaster a perfectly rehearsed smile across her face and she let her expression fall into her natural disdain for the camera crew dirtying up the study around her. On a side table, she saw Willem's phone, already lighting up with Twitter notifications. She grabbed it, input his passcode (6969) and tapped open his notifications screen.

Willem leaned slightly against his desk, accomplishing an uncanny valley kind of laid-back folksiness as he continued. "I don't think I'm alone when I say that this country has lost its way. We were the country that knew if we wanted to be *great*, we had to be *good*. Good to each other." Willem glanced at the floor, a rehearsed break intended to make it seem like what he was reading from the teleprompter was actually off-the-cuff. Chloe raised an eyebrow, impressed. Against all odds, he was almost coming off as human. "It seems like, somewhere along the way, we forgot how to do that," he continued. "We stopped being good to each other, and then we started to blame each other. To lash out. To make each other into villains. We stopped being great, because we stopped thinking we were great." He shook his head. "America used to be the greatest country in the world. And I think we could be again."

Chloe shook her head at Sorkin plagiarizing himself, but figured that no one would notice. She looked at Willem's notifications and saw that, so far, his performance was being praised. A geriatric Hillary Clinton (how was she still alive?) tweeted a clip of the speech with a caption that read "Willem Loots saying what a lot of us have been feeling." His replies were flooded with supportive comments, some surely the botnet that Willem paid to always flood his replies with positivity, but some also definitely from real people.

Willem balled a fist in front of his chest, an attempt at punctuating his words and seeming forceful that Chloe thought looked awkward. "This new tendency to blame, to attack, well, it tore us apart. And that brings me to President Pablo Lopez. He rode into office not from building people up, but by tearing people down. By demonizing people. And not just any people, the people who built this country. The people who built the American dream for themselves, and for all of the rest of us." Willem stopped, scrunching up his face to look like he was holding back tears. Chloe thought it looked more like he was trying to force out a fart, and mentally willed him to stop.

Willem apparently caught her mental wavelength and opened his eyes, looking directly into the camera. "He came for the people of means. The job creators. The architects of the American dream. Can we even imagine what this country would look like if it weren't for men like Andrew Carnegie, Cornelius Vanderbilt, and John D. Rockefeller? If, God forbid, there had been some Pablo Lopez of the 1800s who had been there to stop them before forging this great country in their image? If they had been punished for their lived experience in the same way President Lopez punished Kim Kardashian...."

The official CNNBC account posted a reminder that their retired anchor Anderson Cooper was related to the Cornelius Vanderbilt Willem mentioned in the speech. Hashtags related to the speech were trending nationwide: *#EndLopezHate*, *#Protect-Success*, *#RememberKim*. Chloe remembered just a few months ago when the entire country had watched, salivating, as Kim Kardashian was hung. Now she was a martyr. *What wonderfully fickle people*, she thought. *Gotta love them*.

Loots steeled his face, trying to look serious. "I'm addressing you today, my fellow Americans, because my peaceful, environmentally friendly nation was breached by agents of the American government. These forces include people who worked directly with the President, his chief of staff Lupe Fox, and his senior advisor Javier Potato." Chloe refreshed the feed to see if anyone even noticed him intentionally screwing up Jay's last name—it was all still an outpouring of love, probably no one even knew who Jay was in the first place. "This is an act of *war*. Not just against me, but against my people, against anybody who believes in what America once was. I believe that when you elevate someone like Pablo Lopez, someone who comes to power by drumming up hate, you invite this cycle of chaos and uncertainty. It must end, and it must end today. That is why I am announcing that Loots Town is no longer simply a self-governing Innovation Zone. We are now Loots Nation, a sovereign nation. And we will be working to expand our borders. Because I believe everyone should have the opportunity to live in a country where they have the chance to succeed, and where their head won't be cut off if they do."

There it was. The big swing. If the people were going to turn on him, this is where it would happen. Tentatively, Chloe tapped back onto the feed.

And found that it was still all positive.

Jennifer Lawrence tweeted "Well, I'm moving to Loots Nation" and it already had over 250,000 retweets. *#LootsLiberty* was the top trending topic in the United States. John Cusack tweeted something critical of Loots, and he had already been forced to tweet an apology after he was accused of being racist against South Africans. Willem's replies were flooded with people from everywhere asking when and how they could immigrate to Loots Nation.

Holy fuck, thought Chloe. *We're going to do treason and get away with it. Hunter is going to be so jealous.*

Forty-Four

September 21, 2038 | University of Nevada, Las Vegas

Dima and his soldiers had done a good job at securing the perimeter. There weren't many people left. Sasha met up with him in the parking lot outside the arena where vehicles were filing out.

"All clear, for the most part," Dima said. "And who knows when, or if, this will work. Loots soldiers aren't exactly Navy Seals. The Chechens are the only real fighting force among us." She heard gunshots from the MGM. Dima sighed. "Well, they're fucking themselves over if that makes you feel better." He looked at his shoes.

"Not really," Sasha said. She started to say something, some kind of apology, when Olga of all people walked up.

"Well, well, well," she said, smoking a cigarette. "My shithead niece and nephew who abandoned me for months."

"Olga," Sasha said in alarm. "What are you doing here?"

"Maya wants to see handsome President," Olga said, shrugging.

"Where is she?" Sasha said.

"She climbed over barricade. Wanted picture after event was canceled," Olga said.

"Sasha," Dima said faintly. "Look west." She scanned the

Strip and above the Luxor, she spotted a drone, vibrating like a fart made of metal.

"Jay, it's time," she said to her earpiece. "Everybody!" she yelled as loud as she could. "We need to evacuate! Now! Towards the Fruit Loop," she said, referring to the strip of gay bars nearby. Nobody moved. "Now!" she yelled. She started pushing people north, her eyes on the sky. They looked up.

Pandemonium broke out. She fought her way back to Dima.

"I'll go get Maya," she said.

"No. This is my fuck up," he said, and sprinted towards the arena.

As she herded people out of the Thomas & Mack parking lot, a Loots drone flew directly overhead. Sasha braced for impact.

But the drone sailed on, past the campus. It dropped a missile from the sky, right onto Caesars Palace with a gigantic boom.

Fucking self-driving AI, Sasha thought.

Forty-Five

September 21, 2038 | Loots Town

The timeline had taken a turn. Where Chloe had just a moment before seen nothing but pure adulation, confusion was seeping in. News had broken of a drone strike at Caesars Palace, and now the timeline was littered with live pictures and video updates of pool cabanas in flames and bikini-clad bodies in pieces.

Willem remained on-camera, but his composure was slipping. He twisted up his face, squinting his eye and rubbing his left temple. It dawned on Chloe—his neural implant was feeding him the timeline in real time directly to his brain. When it was positive, it was building him up, but now...

Now this whole thing could turn into a shitshow.

"It's my... It's my understanding that there has been an unfortunate attack right, uhh, right here in Las Vegas. My intelligence, uhhm, indicates that this was an attempt by the anti-Lopez leftists to—" he trailed off, taking a moment to think, then continued "Wait! I mean, this was Lopez himself, the bastard, trying to strike a, *eheuheu*, final strike against capitalism!"

The timeline wasn't buying it, Chloe saw. An account named "LootsTownFlightTracker" had already posted a blown-up photograph of a giant "L" on the drone (Jesus, couldn't this guy do *anything* without stamping his name on it?) along with flight data showing that the drones had taken off from the airfield in Loots Town. Half a million retweets. A data engineer posted a thread explaining how the drone's incorrect course matched a bug in the Pegasus self-driving AI. 250,000 likes. A new hashtag was already trending nationwide: *#LyinLoots.*

Loots self-consciously rubbed his fist against the temple spot above his subdermal implant. *Maybe it wasn't a good idea to put a live feed of the internet in your brain?* Chloe thought. *Who could have guessed?*

"There are now a series of false reports, er, spreading, um, online," Willem said, flailing. "You can't believe, uhh, everything you read on there. This information is clearly being spread by President Lopez, as well as, uhhh," he rubbed at his temples as he tried to think, "as well as haters! There are so many haters out there trying to get me because, uhh, well, because they hate electric cars!"

The American people weren't having it, Chloe could tell from the timeline. A New York Times columnist posted a GIF from *Parks & Recreation* accompanied by a caption saying, "Willem Loots ain't it." President Lopez tweeted a picture of himself safely alongside his aide Javier Betteta with a caption saying his administration would stop at nothing to bring Willem Loots to justice. Jake Tapper quote-tweeted with a solemn thanks to the commander-in-chief. Willem's direct mentions were filling with vitriol and death threats, drowning out all of his paid bots. Videos of Chechens emblazoned with Ls on their uniforms looting Planet Hollywood and throwing tourists into the Bellagio fountains.

Willem, still on camera, seemed increasingly unhinged with the corner of his mouth and his eyelids twitching. "Don't you understand? Don't you people understand? You need *me* more than I need you. I'm rich! I'm the richest man in the world! You, the unwashed masses, need someone like me to take care of you. If you could take care of yourselves, you wouldn't be poor! *Eheuheuheu*!" He stared into the camera, eyes wide, catching his breath. "You all need a daddy! Come to Daddy Willem! *Eheuheuheuheuheuheuheu*!" He doubled over, convulsing with his weird giggle that he couldn't stop.

Chloe knew now that Willem was done. He could have gotten away even with the part where he said poor people needed a Daddy, Americans liked being occasionally degraded as long as it struck them as honest. But the weird giggle on TV was a bridge too far. If there was one thing Americans could never forgive, it was someone being weird and off-putting on TV. The timeline confirmed what Chloe knew instinctively. The clip had already been cut, recut, posted, and re-posted. It was everywhere. Writers who just fifteen minutes ago were singing Willem's praises were now pretending like they had always hated him.

That fickleness could swing both ways. Quick.

Chloe knew now that Willem was cooked. Her chance at being the First Lady of Loots Nation had evaporated with just a few televised seconds of his shrill laughter. She knew Loots Town was probably not long for this world, and that her husband would go down in history as the next Benedict Arnold.

Worse, she was complicit. A screengrab of her standing at Willem's side from the start of his speech had begun to proliferate.

This was going to destroy her personal brand. Unacceptable.

Willem continued grunting and giggling, doubled over against his desk.

Chloe thought quickly and knew what she had to do. His gigantic ivory-handled golden handgun sat on his desk. He put it there to seem "more badass" and like commander-in-chief material.

She shimmied behind the grubby crew guys so that her good side would be facing the camera. She stepped into frame and slid the gun off his table.

She leveled it at his head. He turned to face her, still mid-giggle. "*Eheuheu—*"

She pulled the trigger.

Willem's brain, skull, and blood sprayed the wall of the study.

"You should have restored my social media, prick," she told his dead, convulsing body.

Epilogue

January 14, 2039 | Miami, Florida

Willem stood and held his muscular arms, laughing loudly over an urgent staccato score. A short, serious Chloe with eye wrinkles and side boob looked at him with tears in her eyes. Chloe's eyes flashed back to living in a Ford Bronco with her mother, shivering in the cold, back to Hunter flirting with another woman at their wedding, at the Oligarch holding her in a dilapidated Russian apartment. Back in the present, Chloe's eyes narrowed with resolve as she took the ivory gun from her Dior purse and shot Willem in the face.

He fell to the ground in a handsome heap. Chloe breathed heavily and said, "That was for *democracy*."

Chloe closed the tablet and tossed it on the tile next to her chair. The new Hulu show *Renegade* made Willem more handsome and in order to get a prestige actress to play Chloe, they picked someone old and fat, especially against the muted blues and yellows of the series. If they hadn't paid her 40 million dollars for the rights to the harrowing and mostly true recounting of events in her podcast, *Warrior II with Comrade Chloe,* she would have said no. She was better than TV. She *was* TV.

Her hot pool boy, Paolo, walked up to her with another Mojito. He winked at her. She now lived at the Four Seasons in Miami—the Miami disaster had brought the tide even closer to the newly raised luxury hotel, the rotting streets beneath the surface of the ocean were barely noticeable. She briefly thought that killing somebody would make her feel bad, but it turned out it was the best decision she'd ever made. When her socials were *finally* reinstated after the army released her following the execution, she gained millions of new followers. Sure, they were neckbeard weirdos, but they called her a hero, *Comrade Chloe*, and they had a *lot* of money to spend on her new Patreon. She launched a new athleisure line with yoga pants, sports bras, and t-shirt dresses emblazoned with an outline of Chloe blowing Willem's brains out. Hammer and sickles on apparel made in sweatshops. Whatever. Communism was in.

Whatever the ideology, killing people made money, Chloe understood that. Hell, the Oligarch knew that. Money was death. Death was money. The President understood that when he gave her a medal at the White House. She sipped her mojito, stood, and made eye contact with Paolo. She undid the straps of her bikini and stepped into her plunge pool. Paolo smiled and removed his clothes.

It didn't matter if the actress that played Chloe was ugly. The real Chloe was hotter than she'd ever been.

January 14, 2039 | Washington, D.C.

"And so, intuitively aware of the threat posed by Mr. Loots, you acted unilaterally in gathering information about Loots Town?" the newly minted APP Senator from Colorado peered over her glasses as she questioned Jay from her spot on the absurd Senator dais. A Tweety Bird neck tattoo peeked out from beneath her respectable blouse. "No one at the White House knew about or directed your actions?"

Jay leaned into the thin microphone mounted on the desk in

front of him. "That's correct." He looked good on camera as he sat testifying before the Senate committee, his hair perfectly styled and a new tailored suit on his trim frame.

The Colorado Senator nodded her approval. "Well, Mr. Betteta, I would just like to offer sincere thanks on behalf of myself and my esteemed colleagues that you were there and able to handle the situation before it got even further out of hand. You are a true American patriot." Senators throughout the chamber murmured their assent. "While your actions weren't technically kosher, in my opinion, this nation owes a great debt to you and to Ms. Chloe Thibodeaux." The chamber broke out in applause.

Pablo nodded approvingly to Jay as they watched the coverage on a flatscreen in the presidential residence. "You did good."

Jay, his hair mussed and not quite as perfect as when he was under the lenses of dozens of Senate cameras, couldn't help but grin. He didn't live or die with Pablo's approval anymore, but it still felt good. Pablo. His brother. "Well, it wasn't tough with such friendly questioners," he deflected, "after you managed to pick us up so many seats in the midterms."

"I can't take all the credit there, I think you had something to do with it too," Pablo responded with a wink. After Loots's assassination attempt, Pablo's approval rating had soared to George Bush after 9/11 levels. It turned out that there was nothing like an assassination attempt for presidential popularity. It was perfectly timed for the midterm elections, and the goodwill for Pablo led the APP to huge electoral success.

And Jay had his own success with his promotion to Chief of Staff. Pablo needed a new one after his last one was sent to prison on charges of treason. They watched Lupe on C-SPAN now, in a one-piece orange prison jumpsuit, mumbling answers to grilling from Senators.

"Oof," said Pablo. "They've really got it out for her."

"I wouldn't count her out," responded a woman's voice from the door. It was Sasha Ivanov, the newly hired White

House Press Secretary. "Online chatter is that she looks good in orange. Plus, she's rebranded as a hardcore prison abolitionist."

Jay rolled his eyes, and Pablo caught him. "Look, I'm a prison abolitionist too," he explained, "but in her case, isn't it a little self-serving? How about we abolish prisons *except* for her?"

Pablo laughed. "What do you got?" he asked Sasha.

"We're just about set up for that sit-down with CNNBC."

"Another puff piece?"

She nodded. "Seems like it."

"I'll be right there."

Sasha started to head out the door.

"Oh, one more thing," Pablo called after her. She waited at the door frame. "Any updates on Maya?"

Sasha smiled with a sense of relief. "She's out of surgery and her body is accepting the new pancreas." She pulled out her phone and displayed a picture of a smiling Maya in the hospital, Dima beaming at her side. "Dima's there with her."

Jay felt his eyes moisten but tried to hold it back so his old friend wouldn't think he'd gone soft. Pablo smiled with that wide grin that won him the presidency. "I'm so glad to hear that. I'll be right down."

Sasha nodded and headed out, closing the door behind her, leaving Jay and the President. "There's one other thing," said Pablo. "I've been thinking a lot about what happened last year. And I think I've finally come to a decision. It's time we really killed the rich."

Jay smiled.

The Oligarch watched the American hearings on the death of Willem Loots and tapped his fingers on a mahogany desk that once belonged to Nicholas II of Russia. Americans always thought they were the *first* to do something. His people killed the rich over a hundred years before these buffoons did, and they did it better. They didn't only kill the criminals, they killed their entire families. These Americans believed the symbolism of it all was enough. It wasn't. Humanity was dirtier than that.

Somebody, he knew, would want revenge for the death of Willem Loots. A traitor now, a *victim of political persecution* later.

The phone rang. The Oligarch smiled. Americans were so predictable.

Acknowledgments

First and foremost, thank you to Christoph Paul, Leza Cantoral, Brett Petersen, and everybody at CLASH Books for believing in this book and taking a chance on publishing a novel called Kill The Rich. Thank you to Jake Flores for retweeting our post about the book, and thank you to Max Collins from Eve6 for tagging CLASH. No thanks to Twitter, which we hope will die by the time this book is on shelves.

To Kelly Elcock, Donny Sheldon, Rory Fitzpatrick, Evan Susser, and Robin Snelson, thank you for reading various drafts of this book and providing feedback. Thank you to Joe Milan Jr., Ryan Molloy, Federico Carpio, Lexi Earle, Lizzie Parmenter, Mira Gonzalez, Jason Woliner, and Adam McKay for support and advice. Thanks to Joel Amat Güell for the final cover art and to Cait Raft for the art for the original serialized version.

Thanks to our respective families including Leonora Stephens, Donald Shapiro, Alex Shapiro, Ken Abrams, John Allison, Robin Snelson, and Cary Allison for their unwavering support.

Finally, thank you to Elon Musk and Kim Kardashian, without whom we would not have had the inspiration to write this novel (although any resemblance to actual persons, living or dead, is purely coincidental).

About The Authors

Jack Allison is a Los Angeles-based writer and recipient of a Writer's Guild of America Award. He is the co-host of the podcast *Struggle Session* and former TV writer with credits including *Jimmy Kimmel Live*, *The Academy Awards*, and *Funny Or Die*. Kill the Rich is his debut novel.

Kate Shapiro is a Miami-based writer. She received her MFA in fiction from the University of Nevada, Las Vegas, and holds a BFA from Tisch School of the Arts at New York University. Her work can be seen in *Fence*, *X-R-A-Y*, *HAD*, and *Interim*. *Kill the Rich* is her debut novel.

Also by CLASH Books

DEATH ROW RESTAURANT

Daniel Gonzalez

VIOLENT FACULTIES

Charlene Elsby

EARTH ANGEL

Madeline Cash

BAD FOUNDATIONS

Brian Allen Carr

I, CARAVAGGIO

Eugenio Volpe

DARRYL

Jackie Ess

GAG REFLEX

Elle Nash

LIFE OF THE PARTY

Tea Hacic

GIRL LIKE A BOMB

Autumn Christian

ILL BEHAVIOR

M. Steven S.

Printed in the USA
CPSIA information can be obtained
at www.ICGtesting.com
JSHW021435161023
50269JS00007B/60